DEaDLY BOnD

Louisa Gruber

contents

Chapter 1 - Glittering Snow

"Legend has it that only one white wolf is born each century, and when that white wolf is born, we should all fear for our lives."

I roll my eyes and look around, the entire pack is sitting down in the snow listening closely to the Luna's annual tale about the 'dangerous white wolf.' Half of the pack looks like they are about to faint. The other half tries to pretend that they aren't scared. And then there is me and my mother, we just roll our eyes.

"They are beautiful creatures with a completely white fur, not one single hair is grey or black or brown, their eyes are completely black, just like their blood, but do not get fooled by their appearance, Their bite is deadly, their senses are heightened, and they are almost impossible to kill-"

"Isn't it true that the last white wolf was killed by King Alpha Octavius Winterbourne of the North."Everyone in the pack turn their head to see who the voice might belong to. I quickly spot Jasmine with a raised hand that she lowers when everyone looks at her.

We look up at the Luna again and her face is displaying annoyance, which I'm guessing is caused by the obvious disrespect in Jasmine's voice as she dared to interrupt.

I would be irked too if she spoke to me like that, and I'm not even the Luna.

But regardless of how annoyed our Luna is, she answers with a very calm voice "yes, that is true Jasmine." She opens her mouth to continue her story but Jasmine cuts her off again.

"And he kept its head as a trophy." Her high pitched voice chimes again.

The only reason why they let her talk out of line like that is because she's the betas daughter, if anyone else talked like that to the Luna, we would be put into place.

Suddenly I'm startled as my mother pulls the red hood of my cape over my head earning a few weird glances from our pack. I smack her hand away, and adjust the hood so that it doesn't cover my face.

"Stop it, you're drawing attention." I hiss at the same time as our Luna replies with a yes.

Images of a dead white wolf's head floats my mind and I shiver in disgust.

I need to go run and clear my head...

"When the next white wolf is born every pack of the north, south, east and west will join each other as allies and kill the white wolf, before it kills us all!"

Oh please, If I wanted you dead, I would have killed you all by now...

Only one white wolf is born each century huh? If only they knew.

I take a deep breath again, I can't let my anger get the better of me. Then I would be everything they say I am...

"You are all dismissed." She finally says.

I look up to see everyone standing up and walking back to where they came from, going on about their usual business in the village

I gaze over at my mother and she gives me a sad smile, she's been giving me a lot of those lately, almost as if she knows something bad is bound to happen but I shake it off and ignore the feeling of dread.

She interlocks her arm with mine and we begin to walk towards our home.

"Willow."

A voice calls from behind and a hand grabs my shoulder shortly after.

I turn around quickly in a defesnive manner causing my mother to let go of my arm. My eyes land on Aaron the alphas son, who's hand is quickly retreating, my reaction probably surprised and confused him.

"Um sorry Willow, I just haven't seen you in a few days, I just wanted to say hi." He says in a soothing tone.

"Sorry." I look down in embarrassment. "The story just got me all scared and jumpy." I laugh awkwardly and look up again, Aaron looks at me and smiles. His hair almost looks like the color of a tree, and his eyes look like leafs in the forest when they aren't covered completely in snow.

I immediately calm down, he's always had that effect on me, that's probably why my mother likes him so much. And I'm not going to lie, I guess I've always liked him too. For a while I even thought he would be my mate... but that was back when I was naive.

We look at each other smiling for a few moments before my mother breaks the silence. "You know what, you can come home later, I'll just go ahead."

I turn my head and give her a half-smile and then she turns around and walks away leaving me and Aaron behind.

I turn back to Aaron and remove my hood now feeling more comfortable in my skin.

"Scary story isn't it?" He asks and gestures for me to walk besides him with a quick nod of his head, I quickly follow suit and we start slowly moving through the village.

"Yes." Is all I say.

He gives me a sideways glance and a smirk, "but it is just a story."

I frown puzzled by his words. "What do you mean?"

He stops in his tracks and I do as well following his move and he shrugs in an unbothered manner, "I just don't believe that story."

As one of his hands grabs onto a lock of my white hair I stand completely still. Aaron looks deep in thought as he examines the hair. I should move away, I think, but I just stand there looking at him dumbfounded.

He lets go after a few seconds. My eyes follow as he looks at his fingers in complete silence, his lips slowly form a smile and he finally looks at me again.

"I'll see you later." He says whilst walking away with a subtle smile.

"See you later." I reply quietly watching his retreating form.

•~•~•~•~•~•~•~•~•

I am running...

In the end of the forest where no sane wolf would go. It's so beautiful, yet so dangerous.

It's no one's territory, therefore it's super dangerous as there aren't any laws here. Any wolf could kill me, and they wouldn't be breaking any law whatsoever, but it isn't me that should be scared...

Their bite is deadly... my legs begin to hurt.

The last white wolf was killed... My lungs are burning.

He kept its head as a trophy... My eyes are coal black.

I begin to slow down as my anger starts leaving my body. I stop running completely when I see the little lake in between the snow covered trees. The lake looks magical in the middle of the white forest, it's green color stands out and looks almost a little too inviting.

I know this forest, I've been here a thousand times. It's the only place I can let my wolf be free without fear.

I place my red dress that I had been carrying in my mouth next to the lake. I scan the dress for any rips that my teeth might have caused while I carried it, luckily I only find a few.

I look down at the reflection in the water of the lake. Completely white fur, black eyes and pointy ears are reflected in the lake. I am looking at my wolf. Right now it would be easy for anyone to see who the white wolf is. That's why I'm running in the dangerous forest, the chance of meeting someone here is very small, and even if I did I'd be able to outrun them and my presence would be nothing but a hallucination. You would have to be an idiot, or a very powerful wolf to come here.

I dip my head down and drink a bit of water to ease the burning in my throat. It's strange that the water hasn't frozen completely with all this snow around. Again... a magical lake.

When I feel like the water has eased the pain in my throat enough I look around. Left then right. No one is here. Good.

I begin to shift back, my bones start cracking into place. In less then a few seconds I'm back in my human form.

My body is still heating up, and the snow isn't cooling it down like I had hoped it would. In an attempt to cool myself I walk into the lake slowly, still leaving my red dress behind. This helps, and I breathe through my nose slowly enjoying the silence. As I swim in the lake I feel vulnerable and alone but it's not a bad feeling per-say, it's actually what I'm used to.

I'll always be alone with this secret looming over me...

The feeling of being alone doesn't last long though, instead it's replaced by an irrational thought. I feel as if the forest has grown eyes and is watching my every move.

I sigh feeling irritated that my moment alone was ruined and within minutes I'm out of the water, putting on my red dress. Then I begin to walk around on my human legs feeling slightly more refreshed, looking at the beauty of the dangerous forest.

My fingers run over the trees as I walk amongst them and my bare feet leave footprints in the glittering snow. The mist hides the forest well, and the only way to see more of it is to walk through, but if you do so the mist will hide where you just came from, deleting your tracks and concealing your presence.

I walk further into the forest completely in a trance by the beautiful forest. My senses are occupied with the peacefulness of the nature, yet the creeping feeling of eyes following me around doesn't quite seem to go away either. Perhaps there's more to the forest than I was aware of.

I reach the edge of the forest, only to find a lack of thick mist and a wide gap between where I'm standing and another forest edge. Snow covers every bit of the open field, making the gap look magical.

I've never gone this far, I must've been really angered. Perhaps this also explains the odd feeling.

Suddenly my senses heighten, as I hear thuds of paws against the ground. Four... wait no. five wolves.

Then a pleasant scent hits my nostrils, a scent of fresh air, not like the smell of outside, more like the scent of fresh air on the top of a mountain, the type that reaches all the way down your lungs, and clears out any worry you might have in that moment. My trance is broken when I hear growls, but by then it's too late...

Five wolves step out of the other forest edge on the opposite side of me. The one in the front approaches with an alpha-like power, he makes the other wolves look small in comparison. His fur is black, completely black in fact.

How peculiar.

I've never seen a wolf who is completely black.

My mind must be playing a trick on me.

I analyze the black wolf further, his eyes are glowing silver and they look enchanting as he scans me. The scent thickens the closer he gets. He is taking powerful strides towards me with the other wolves following obediently behind.

The scent must be coming from him.

The brown and gray wolves behind him stop walking, but he moves a few more steps in front of them before he also comes to a halt in the glittering snow.

While still having a great distance between us I grow anxious that they've moved closer.

What should I do?

If I shift now they'll know I'm the white wolf and I can't risk that even if I can outrun them they've seen my human form. There are also five witnesses, and they all look quite powerful especially the black wolf who exudes incomparable power. I could probably kill all the brown and gray wolves, but something about that black wolf tells me that he'll be harder to kill, plus I don't want to kill anyone... Maybe if I just talk in a calm manner I can get out of this. Surely not everyone are murderous.

"I do not want trouble." My voice is low, but I know that they can all hear me clearly. Their ears peak up slightly at my voice.

It is dead silent. Not even a bird in the sky dares to whistle, and all I can hear is the growing intensity of my heartbeat.

The black wolf looks at me with piercing eyes, and for the first time we gain direct eye contact. I feel an electrical surge of energy rush through me upon letting his eyes so I look away in a hurry afraid of the feeling.

When no one growls or takes another step I slowly turn to leave in hopes that the silence means my request of no trouble is accepted. But the Alpha snaps his jaw in an aggressive manner as if saying, "take another step, I dare you."

I turn back immediately and stand still frustrated that I cannot just leave. I look around for an escape though, only to find none. What could they possibly want with me?

The four wolves behind the Alpha also look at me, but no one does anything. So I do the most stupid thing out of panic...

I run...

I run in my human form, because I still can't risk being caught as the white wolf. Realistically I know I can't outrun them like this but I'm currently not driven by logic, it's pure instinct.

I run in my slightly ripped red dress and bare feet.

I run away from the enchanting smell.

I run as I hear the howl of the Alpha and the loud continuing thuds, as the other wolves paws hit the ground while they run after me.

My legs begin to hurt and my chest starts burning. The smell isn't fading at all either and I know what that means. It means they're closing in on me so I make the mistake of looking back, to see how far they are from me.

They're almost right behind me and when I turn my head back to look where I'm running, it's too late... A tree blocks my view, and I try to throw myself to the side to avoid impact. I fall down as I lose my balance, and roll four times in the snow.

I huff in pain while quickly trying to get up by pushing my arms and knees against the ground. But I immediately get pushed down by a paw half the size of my head.

I can hear the wolves growling and I turn my head a little. The dark brown wolf is pushing me down, while the three other wolves stand behind him. The alpha is nowhere to be seen.

I try to slow my breathing down and I say with a raspy voice, "please let me go I-"

The dark brown wolf snaps his jaw at me. And I shut my mouth. I really shouldn't be this scared but I've never dealt with this kind of trouble before.

All of a sudden the fresh scent grows thicker, and I try my best to look around while being pressed to the ground.

My eyes finally spot the Alpha walking through the mist and towards us, but he isn't a wolf anymore. He is a muscular man wearing nothing but pants in the midst of putting on a shirt, with black hair, silver eyes and olive skin.

His human form!

The other wolves back up a bit, and the paw on my back is removed as he also retreats.

As the man approaches his eyes begin to glow again and before I can question it my vision becomes clearer as I feel the electrical surge of energy course through me again. I realize my eyes are glowing too through my clear vision. The world has never looked so clear.

Then it feels like a string pulls at my heart, then a thousand strings pull at my heart, but it doesn't hurt at all. I slowly push myself up, and when I'm finally standing steady, he stops right in front of me and his eyes stop glowing, just like mine.

"I have to go." My voice is shaky, and I'm panicking.

His eyes snap to mine. "No." His tone is final.

I begin to look around in panic, I have to get away!

In theory I should be able to kill them all, but if they have more men and women waiting to fight, they might warn others. I just can't risk it! And that black wolf seems strangely and unexplainably powerful. It honestly frightens me a bit.

I have to talk my way out of this.

"Look at me!" A velvet-like voice says sternly.

I slowly turn my head, but when my eyes find him, I quickly snap my head down to look at my bare feet in an attempt to avoid his intense gaze. His eyes are truly mesmerizing.

"I said look. at. me." He is getting impatient. Good, maybe I can annoy him so he'll let me go.

I keep my eyes locked on the ground.

Not a good idea because he takes yet another step towards me. I gasp and take a step back, but my back touches a tree. I'm trapped!

"Stop." I say and get the courage to look him in the eyes.

He tilts his head a little with a smirk on his... beautiful lips, and his eyes are beautiful too, and his lips-

"No." His voice cut off my wandering thoughts.

Wait what... lips?!

"No, what?" I question as I already forgot what we were talking about.

He takes another step and stops right in front of me with a distance so small only air can fit between, he's still smirking. He finds this amusing?

I shake my head, breaking whatever trance I was in. I will not stand here and be humiliated.

"Let me go!" I say again with a new found courage.

"No."

Is that all this man can say?

So I do another stupid thing inspired by my newfound rage... I punch him. Or I try at least. Just as my hand is about to collapse with his face, he catches it. Electricity sparks between us.

How did he do that? I'm too fast for most people!

He quickly locks my hand against the tree behind me. "Don't you know who I am?"

My cheeks flash red and I look down, he's standing a little too close for comfort, yet somehow it's comforting. "Am I supposed to?"

He lets out a small laugh, while the wolves snort behind him. "Look up."

And just like that I do.

Our eyes connect.

His eyes glow once again, just as mine do.

That's when our voices meld together in one word, while our hearts are pulled toward each other, and sparks fly free between us, connecting us.

In unison we come together as one voice. "Mate."

_______________________________________A/N

Hi guys, this is actually a story I wrote a long time ago when I was younger, but I never published it sadly, however I am now! (Plus I'm adding some more stuff to make it more interesting and also just editing through it all)

I love feedback and I'd love to hear from you all, so don't be scared to leave a message!

Also don't forget to vote (aka click the star) if you liked it, as it helps a lot and I'd really appreciate the support<3

Hopefully I'll see ya again, bye for now.

CHAPTER 2 - Farewell

Mate?! What? The word rings in my ears.

No this can't be. I am a white wolf, and according to the legend only a white wolf can get a mate if they contain around the same amount of power... or if they are a white wolf.

And he is certainly not a white wolf.

I shiver thinking about his completely black fur.

I look him up and down.

How much power is he containing?

His grip tightens around my hand. It appears he's not too fond of me questioning whether or not he is my mate.

And yet I can't help but frown my eyebrows while saying, "this can't be." My voice is dripping with disbelief.

There's a sharp intake of breath, then in less than a second his mouth is right next to my shoulder.

I'm too slow to react as I stand there like a deer caught in headlights.

My reflexes must be slow because of him.

I'm frozen.

His fresh scent has me in a spell.

And somehow his presence is calming yet intense at the same time.

I'm pulled back to reality when he breathes in my scent. He lets a satisfied exhale escape his lips and I catch a faint whisper from him that sounds like "it is true."

"You are mine." He then says sternly, while letting his mouth hover over my shoulder. I can literally feel his words on my shoulder.

"No I'm not!" I shoot back in protest without much thought.

Anyone standing near us can feel his anger radiating off him as I say that.

But instead of yelling at me, he lets his lips grace the skin where my neck and shoulder connect. Confidently letting his lips hover there.

My eyes glow again, while my body fills with anticipation and electricity. What's happening?

And that's when I remember something through my clouded mind. The bite of your mate is a step closer to sealing the bond.

My heart picks up it's pace as I realize that this does in fact confirm our bond.

His teeth teasingly touch the skin near my shoulder, and the act feels like a splash of water to my face.

I an instant push him away easily and he stumbles a bit due to him being caught off guard.

I must have an effect on him too.

At first he looks confused as I just broke his daze, but then his jaw tightens and his eyes turn dark in an instant. He tries to walk up to me again, but I step away from him and the tree.

He stops and tilts his head in challenge.

Then he takes one more step.

I take a step back. "Stop." My stern voice travels through the forest.

He stops and tightens his jaw with so much force it looks like his teeth might break. "Show your King respect." His voice is cold, as his eyes dark with a booming storm.

King? He doesn't look that old.

How old is my mate?

I cringe "You're king Octavius?" I question looking at him with resentment while flashes of a decapitated white wolf runs through my mind.

No one has heard from him in a while. And I doubt that this is him. And if it is… I'm truly in a lot of danger.

"No." He speaks up angered. "I'm King Legion Winterbourne." His voice is now pure power and pride.

Realization settles in me. That's why no one has heard from Octavius.

"Your father is dead?" My voice is softer now feeling slightly scared to speak out of line. Dead parents tend to be a sensitive subject and given his current mood I doubt I should push my luck.

"Yes, so show your King and mate respect." He's clearly running out of patience. It also seems clear that he's more pissed off about the fact that I'm trying to deny him as my mate than the death of his father.

Even though it's awful, I can't help but be happy that King Octavius is dead. He was a threat to my existence. I try to contain my smile.

But then my blood runs cold in an instant, and the fleeting joy I've discovered evaporates as swiftly as it emerged.

My mate is the son of the last person who killed a white wolf.

And again, I panic.

I don't know what to do.

I can't run.

I can't shift.

I can't be his mate.

My heart beats faster again, I can hear it pound in my ears.

He looks intensely at me as he analyses my body language. He must hear it too.

My brain is hurting trying to find a loophole out of this. That's when I find it.

I once heard about a man who rejected his mate, it is supposed to be very painful but maybe I can reject him. It feels like my only choice.

"I don't want you as my mate." My heart pinches a little when I say that. And Legion looks at me like he wants to kill me. In three quick steps he's in front of me. The scent of him is slowly repairing my heart again. Then he lifts me in a swift movement and throws me over his shoulder.

At first I'm dumbfounded, but then I look at my surroundings, which isn't a lot. His back, the ground, and that's it!

"What are you doing, put me down!" I sound weird and raspy upside down, but I believe my point comes across.

He begins to walk away with me. "What are you doing?" And even though I know it's going to hurt, I say, "I reject y-"

In a quick thud I'm on the snowy ground. Thankfully he dropped me in a thick pile of snow and not an ounce of pain came with the fall, almost as if on purpose... "You can't reject me, you are mine." He looks like he is on the verge of going on a killing spree. But instead of killing anyone he chooses a different unexpected approach.

He kneels in front of me and grabs my hand. Electricity runs through us, connecting us and it feels as if this is what I've been missing my entire life. I've been missing him.

My heart warms up and is pulled towards him again. Our eyes light up. He places my hand on his heart, I look him in the eyes that are slightly covered by his black hair. He looks vulnerable, hurt even, I don't want him hurt, and I don't know why. I just know that I can feel his sadness somehow. His sadness is deep... it's real.

"You're mine and I'm yours." His voice breaks a little, it's barely noticeable but I hear it nonetheless.

His heart has the same rhythm as mine now. He looks into my eyes. "What's your name?" His voice is soft.

I take a deep breath and answer feeling responsible for his sadness. "Willow Ashen."

"Willow Ashen." He speaks my name with such ease it sounds perfect when he says it. I want him to say it again.

He removes my hand from his heart and I feel lost for a second. He takes my hand and helps me up slowly. "Do you live near here?" His voice is enchanting and velvety. I'm mesmerized yet again.

I nod twice quickly as if I can't help but answer his every word.

"Good, you will get an hour to say goodbye to your family and pack, we have a long journey ahead of us."His words startle me.

"What?" And just like that I'm pulled back to reality again and the sweet moment is over.

His jaw tighten again. "You are my mate and you're coming with me." His tone leaves no room for questions. Well that was it on the vulnerability I guess.

"But-"

He smells the air and begins to walk toward my village, dragging me along by the wrist.

He could smell my village from here?!

He can't be a regular wolf.

We walk toward my village, all five of us, with the wolves in the background and Legion with me in the front.

I figure that the best thing to do is to walk back with them, it's not like I can run away. Where would I go? Maybe my mother knows what to do.

His hand is holding my wrist. Securing me in place, hoping that I won't run away. His touch feels good, like this is indeed what I've been missing. I've always seen people from my village find their mate, but that's when they are around 18, not 20 like me, I don't even know Legions age. I take a quick peek at him, his black hair shines in the sun, his silver eyes are powerful and breathtaking and his lips are full. He is handsome.

I never thought I was going to get a mate, I've always known that your mate must match your power in some way or another, and I always thought no one could match any of mine, but he has proved me wrong. I wonder where his power lay. As I walk back to the village it is with mixed emotions of fear and also a feeling I can't quite out my finger on, I just know it feels strangely good.

•~•~•~•~•~•~•~•~•~•

"This is your village?" You can almost hear the disbelief in his voice. He's probably used to the luxury life in his kingdom. My village isn't poor though, it's simply small and cozy. He is just being a pretentious snob.

"Yes." I rip my hand out of his hold and he looks alarmed at me. "Relax, I'm capable of walking myself."

He rolls his eyes, "that's not what I fear."

I let out a huff. "I know." And walk away without him. He's behind me in seconds following my every move. He's more alert now that his wolves aren't with him. He told them to wait by the edge of the forest. I can't even imagine people's reactions if they'd see me walking with five unknown guys four of which in their wolf forms.

People around us start to notice that something is off, they obviously don't recognize King Alpha Legion as from around here and we only ever hear stories about the royals, no one from the village has ever met one... well besides me. They whisper to each other and point to our direction discreetly, but I see it because of my powerful senses. I wonder if Legion notices it too. They look very alarmed, we are not used to outsiders here. More and more people stop to watch us walk by... if only they knew they were in the presence of the King... Well... also a white wolf.

I tune into some of the whispers, "Who is he?" "Do you recognize him?" "Should we tell Alpha." The last one makes me snort as he is the Alpha of all.

Legion leans down a bit. "Do you live far from here?" He sounds impatient, I bet the curious swarms of people are starting to annoy him.

Just when I'm about to answer, my name is called out from the crowd. "Willow?"

I look over to where I heard my name being called and I see Aaron walk in my direction with a worried expression plastered across his face.

"It's fine." I quickly say to not create a bigger scene and because I sense an immediate tensing of Legion. I just need to get home to my mother, she'll know what to do.

He doesn't listen to me though and stops in front of us. I feel some kind of anger washing over me, but it isn't mine... I look to Legion and he looks about ready to bite Aarons head off.

"She said it was fine." Legion's voice isn't loud at all yet everyone stops talking, even the dumbest wolf would be able to sense his power.

Aaron is caught off guard as well and he takes a small step back, but then he realises his action and takes a step forward again.

In less than a heartbeat I'm being pushed behind Legion and it's like everyone stops breathing, including me.

I quickly step away from him and rush in the middle of them again holding up a hand to signal them to hold on before someone does something rash. I turn to Aaron as I know him fully. Legion is still unknown to me and I don't know how to talk to him yet. "We're just going to my house, that's all Aaron." I try to look like I'm not as nervous as I actually am.

Aaron, who isn't looking at me at all, is having a staring contest with Legion, but after a bit he finally looks at me. "Who is he?" His question is seething through his teeth and I find it sensible since no one has seen him before and Aaron is probably assuming the worst due to his protective nature.

But again before I can get a word in, someone shouts something from afar. We all turn to see the Alpha of the village walk over to us. He's also Aaron's father.

"What is all this about?" He tries to sound dominant but I can understand why that's difficult in Legion's presence.

Alpha Greg walks in front of his son. He tries to look intimidating with his brown eyes. The brown eyes that match his brown grayish hair. "Who are you?" He questions out loud catching everyone's attention in case it had slipped a bit since we walked in, though I doubt it.

Without giving it anymore thought I answer with the truth. "He's my mate." My words mute the entire village fully.

Legion is fuming, I can sense it, but there's a second where he's also proud as I announce that he's my mate.

I look over to Aaron to see his reaction. His face has lost all color with a shocked expression forming on his face. I can't help but feel bad, I just don't know why. I want to reach out to him and hug him, so I take a step towards him, before I can walk any further I feel a strong grip around my arm pulling me back.

I turn to Legion to tell him to let me go, but before I even say anything, he sends me a look that tells me that I shouldn't test his patience right now. He also shoots Aaron a threatening look as if telling him to back up.

Suddenly we're moving again. Legion's walking away from the alpha while dragging me along, the entire village follows us with their eyes as I follow Legion because I don't want to cause more problems. Even though I know Legion doesn't want me so much as looking at Aaron right now, I can't help but let my eyes wander, he looks like someone has died. Like I died. The only thing keeping me from running to him, telling him that everything will be alright, is Legion. His grip isn't hurting me but it's strong enough for me to get the message. Surprisingly enough though the alpha isn't stopping us. Perhaps he also senses a power that he can't compete with.

We come to a halt at the end of the village after walking in silence and with a looming rage hanging over us and Legion turns to me. "Which way?" He asks, looking back at the village.

"Not much further" I sigh. "Just down that path." I point to the right with the hand that he hasn't restrained.

"But the village ends here." He says while analyzing me with skeptical eyes.

I roll my eyes and shake my head. "I'm not lying, my mom and I live just outside the village." I sound just as annoyed as I am.

He looks at me for a second to see if im telling the truth before walking in the direction I pointed out.

And just as I said, we arrive at my house before long. "You live here?" At his comment I snap quickly.

"Yes why?!" But when I look at him he looks confused by my small outburst.

"Why are you not living within your own village?" He says as if it's obvious. Which to be fair it is but it has been a long day and the day isn't even over.

"Oh...." I trail off. He can't know the real reason, which is my mothers need for privacy due to her fear of me being exposed as the white wolf. "We just like the quiet." I lie.

He doesn't look like he's buying it but before he can aks more questions I rip my arm out of his hold and walk up to my door and knock. He just lets me. Now normally I wouldn't knock but by doing this I hope it'll alert my mother and she'll know something is wrong before I burst in with an unknown man.

I bet that's not exactly a mothers dream. Oh this man? It's just my mate I found in the forest, oh and he's also the new king, oh and the son of King Octavius... Anyways say hello and then goodbye as I'm being forced to leave... that is unless you have a plan which I really hope you do...

As I stand there lost in my thoughts it takes me a moment to realize that no one has answered my knocks. I try again and I hear Legion sigh behind me. Again, nothing. Frustrated and worried I open the door, not a single candle is lit and the presence of my mother is lacking. "Hello." I try as I walk inside, Legion follows me.

"Are your parents not home?" I cringe at the word parents.

"Just mother." I simply say. But it gets the point across and Legions voice soften as he says, "I see". Dead parents is indeed a sensitive subject.

He waits in the doorway as I scan the rest of my house, I'm guessing to block a possible escape route.

There's no sign of my mother but I'm not particularly alarmed that my she isn't home just annoyed by the timing as I really need her right now. My guess is she went to our forest to clear her head as well as I did, she'd usually go on small walks. All of a sudden Legion speaks up, "pack your bags Willow."

I'm taken aback by my name coming from his mouth but continue pacing around nonetheless to seem busy and to stall time. I ignore his command and I can see form the corner of my eye that he continues to watch me carefully. "My patience only goes so far." He breaks the silence again now sounding more serious than before.

I don't respond this time either but I stop pacing and dare to look in his direction in a somewhat discreet manner. He looks stoic standing there with his arms crossed leaning against the doorframe, but it won't be long until he'll lose whatever patience he somehow has for me. I bet kings aren't used to waiting...

I start pacing again and he sighs. "If you don't want to pack then I don't see why I should wait any longer." His voice makes me anxious, I don't know if it's because of his unexplainable power or because of the bond but it makes me feel a type of vulnerable I'm not used to so I retaliate.

"You're right you shouldn't, you should go." Not much thought goes into my statement besides my annoyance with the whole situation and before I can think much further of it, I'm pinned against a wall.

"Don't test me Willow, you don't know what I'm capable of." His mouth is right next to my ear and his body is pressed up against mine keeping me in place. "I could've made you come with me right when I found you or I could make you go now before you get a chance at a farewell, and none of which has happened... yet, so choose your next words carefully."

_______________________________A/N

Hey again, hope you liked chapter 2!

As always leave a comment to let me know what you think:)

Don't forget to vote!

Chapter 3 will be ready soon enough.

CHAPTER 3 - DEPARTURE

My heart is pounding in my chest as I stand there pinned between Legion and the wall. I feel frightened by the sudden action and strangely enough I'm also filled with a lust that I quickly suppress.

The dang bond is messing with my head, the second he touches me my body starts betraying me!

"It must be a mistake!" I speak out finally. "I can't be yours." I sound pathetic and small but it also feels freeing to voice my thoughts.

How can someone like me have a mate… not to mention the freaking king!

He takes a small step back so my body is able to move whilst still standing way too close, so I keep my head down to avoid his eyes.

"Do you not understand what the bond means Willow?" He retorts sternly.

"I do! But you are the king and I am me! This does not make sense, don't you see it's a mistake of some kind." Frustrated I throw my hands over my face. It doesn't take long before I feel his hands grab mine and he nudges my hands a bit signalling me to remove them from my face, but instead of doing so I press them harder against my head.

Suddenly I feel cold and I can sense that he has fully left my proximity, however I don't remove my hands to check as I now feel embarrassed by my discomposure. If I hide in my hands I'm sure he'll get the hint and leave... Right...?

Probably not.

My head peaks up as I hear rummaging, Legion isn't to be seen anywhere so I follow the sound. The sounds are coming from my room and I find him there throwing clothes on my bed. "What are you doing." I almost screech out.

He doesn't even bother turning around, he just carries on as he speaks up with his back turned, "you don't really need much of this cheap clothes, back at the castle you'll have what you need, so just clothes for the trip will do."

I panic and now it's my turn to grab his arm to stop him. "I'm not leaving like this!" He yoinks my arm effortlessly and I fall into the bed. "Then tell me how you are leaving." He snaps.

As I lay there I feel disoriented as ever. If he truly is my mate... then being apart will hurt me tremendously, but my life is in danger if I stay with him because I'm the white wolf.

Part of me wants to follow my mate everywhere, I suppose that's what a mate does to you, but the other part of me can't allow it because of the danger it entails.

I feel tears form in my eyes under his scrutinizing gaze but I don't allow a single tear to drop. My chest rises with each breath I take and breathing seems harder than it should. Today did not go as I expected...

He towers over me while I'm on the bed, his face is expressionless and I start to question if he even has real emotions.

"Hello?" We both turn our heads in sync to my mothers voice but none of us speak a word. She must've heard the news by now and I push myself up to sit on the edge of my bed as I hear my mothers footsteps approach the bedroom door.

She rounds the corner and a shocked facial expression fills her face. "Oh my... it is true then." She sounds just as worried as I feel and more anxiety rises within me as I start to doubt if anything can be done. I know The Moon Goddesses' will shouldn't be questioned but I don't understand her plan right now.

My mother stands still not saying a thing and the silence that washes over us is thick enough to cut with a knife. Legion breaks the silence, "your daughter is here to say goodbye." And with that he walks past my mother leaving the bedroom.

My mother immediately becomes wide-eyed as he passes her and it's obvious that she doesn't quite know what to say, her mind is racing and she ends up shooting me a questioning look.

I hear the front door close and I know he has left my house, it is just me and my mother now.

She blinks a few times in confusion and utter one word. "Willow?"

After I explain everything, all from my adventure in the forest- of course leaving out the fact that I was running in my wolf form scared Legion might be listening in on our conversation-, to Legion being the king and to the demand that I leave today with Legion, my mother has a slight melt down.

Since I can remember, it has just been me and her and the thought of leaving must be causing her just as much pain as it's causing me, but she explains to me that there's nothing she can do, against the royals we have no power, besides she underlines that he is my mate, as she explains that mates aren't a thing to take lightly.

She also tries to look at the bright side focussing on the fact that I did indeed have a mate which we never thought to be possible, but then she realizes the same thing as I did... that he must possess similar power as me and her face grows pale and her look becomes distant.

She looks like she's about to faint before she mutters that I must reject him. The word spoken ever so quietly is dangerous and in what feels like a heartbeat Legion is behind my mother with blackened eyes, but he's not alone. The four other wolves stand behind him, now in their human form.

"We are leaving now!" His voice is loud and clear. He walks past my mother again ignoring her cries and grabs my upper arm. And as he drags me out of my bedroom like some disobedient puppy, my mother hurries after us apologizing saying that she understands his reaction but she means nothing by it. She proclaims it is just a dramatic reaction as this is all confusing to her.

She tries to beg more but notices that he doesn't budge, as she does this I try to resist his hold but that doesn't budge either. I note that his hold is somehow tight enough to where I can't free myself but not so tight as to bruise me or hurt me, it's a fine balance that he manages to walk.

Once we are by the exit with no luck of convincing him to let me go my mother runs over and tries to peel his hands off my arm, his four men that were once behind us all like guards are now on my mother dragging her away and I yell. "STOP! PLEASE!" My voice must've sounded urgent or important enough to listen to as everyone stops dead in their tracks. "I'll go with you but please let me say a proper goodbye to my mother and I'll pack a bag." I urge looking pleadingly at Legion who is starring straight ahead.

He has a rage filled aura surrounding him as he stands there in silence and his men, who are still holding my mom in place await his answer. He takes a deep breath. "You have one hour." He hisses and lets go. His men let my mother go and follow shortly after.

•~•~•~•~•~•~•~•~•~•~•

Packing my bag feels surreal, like this is all just a bad dream. My mother cries as she helps me and tries to stay optimistic by explaining how a mate is truly a blessing even if it doesn't feel like it right now. She doesn't mention directly the danger I'm being put in, but she does remind me to wear my hood many times as a discreet warning to what we both know could be the death of me if discovered.

The rest of my packing is a blur, and at some point in that blur I finish my packing, hug my mother goodbye and cry while promising to see her again some day. She says a lot I don't hear but I try to find strength in me to flash her a reassuring smile whenever I can even through the tears. She walks me out where Legion is standing ready to depart. She hugs me one final time and whisper "I love you." I try to say it back but nothing come out but a pathetic broken sound, she hugs me even tighter in her embrace. "I know." Those are the last words she speaks as Legion takes my bag and pass it on to one of the men, then he places his hand on my lower back and guide me away from my home... My whole life... Everything I've ever known...

As we walk through the village for one last time we gain a lot of attention as expected. People are still whispering and many seems almost to be in awe by Legion. The crowd is filled with familiar faces I've known my whole life and I even spot Jasmine in the crowd. She's glaring daggers at me but it doesn't surprise me, just Jasmine being Jasmine.

I'll add her to the list of people I won't miss.

Just as I finish that thought I notice Aaron pushing his way through the mass of people, who are pretending to mind their business while making it obvious that they're not. I know he's here to say goodbye or protest or do some sort of thing that won't be appreciated by Legion so I try to shake my head at Aaron hoping he'll get my hint. He does not. He walks up to us and blocks our path. "Are you okay?" he insists.

Legions hand leaves my back as he steps in front of me. His men back him up by stepping a bit forward as well while still staying behind us both. "She is fine." He shoots back.

"I wasn't talking to you." Aaron is quick to snap.

My stomach drops. Bad idea.

Legion sighs. "Is that how you speak to your king?"

The crowd goes dead silent. So silent that if someone dropped a pin it could be heard.

My view is limited as I stand behind Legion, normally I would react more but my recent separation with my mother seems to have placed me in a numb state.

"My king please understand that my son is just worried for his friend." Another voice speaks up. I peak from behind Legion and see that it is Luna Elena. Behind her stands her very worried husband and pack Alpha.

"I do not care who is speaking, you will do it with respect." Legion speaks up again. I peak at Aaron as well and he's already looking at me.

"My son didn't realize he was speaking to the king, we apologize." Alpha Greg chimes in.

Luna Elena speaks again. "We are-"

She doesn't get to finish her sentence before Aaron interrupts again. "Let me speak to Willow."

I can practically feel the heat radiating off Legion as he closes his hands and before this escalates further I put my hand on his closed fist. The action gains his attention and he throws a side eye my way. I don't say anything but a fresh set of tears are streaming down my cheeks and I feel his hands loose their anger ever so slightly.

I take a chance and I walk past him with timid steps. Surprisingly he lets me and I take the opportunity to walk up to Aaron, pressing my luck further. Even more to my surprise he lets me but a feeling that doesn't belong to me tugs at my core. I ignore it and stop in front of Aaron.

"I'm okay." I lie. It's obvious but I try to hide my pain nonetheless.

Aarons lifts his hand to my face and I hear Legion sucking in air but instead of touching my face Aaron clasps a lock of my hair. "I know."

It's like he knows...

I start to bawl after his words are spoken and throw myself into his arms. It's unexpected for everyone including me and I allow myself to enjoy his embrace one last time. He holds onto me as if he'll never let go. But this is unfortunately not the case. Barely any time passes before I understand my action and I let go before Legion or his men have a chance to walk up to us.

I sniffle and return to Legion who appears to be fuming under his stoic expression, as a response to my action, but I keep my head down and prepare myself for him to grab my arm again upon my return, bracing for a grip rough enough to bruise me this time. But he does not. Instead he walks past me and says "let's go."

And we all follow. We follow until the village is nothing but a sand-corn in the distance between the trees of the deep forest. Back where it all started...

_______________________________________ A/N

Here's yet another chapter! Hope it was just as great as the others (if you even thought that haha).

Don't forget to vote aka click the star, it helps my story a lot!

Next chapter will be ready soon:)

CHAPTER 4 - MOUNTAINS

The silence is deafening. Since we left my village, not a word has been spoken and I've just kept my head down. I don't want to talk to Legion, talking to him feels like betraying myself. Like I'm somehow accepting the situation, and even if I understand the necessity of it all, I'm far too stubborn to speak up. Besides I don't know what to say.

His four men are now walking a bit in front of us, as if to protect their king by going first or perhaps just to give us privacy, I'm not sure, but I'm leaning towards the first seeing as Legion has yet to utter another word to me.

I've started to analyze the men. The one who appears to be the leader of the four, outside of Legion of course, has brown reddish hair, I've deducted that he might be the beta. Another is blonde and the two others are brunettes, one having a lighter shade than the other.

They're all of similar build, by that I mean everyone of them has a clear strength as I'm guessing you'd need a good physique to be able to travel so far, but they all vary in height.

I know that the kingdom is far north, and although we're part of the north I'm still guessing the trip will take at least a week, and that's counting running in wolf form... which I cannot do.

But like I said the silence is just excruciating. I try to focus on my feet as they leave their usual prints in the snow and as my dress drags along. I'm wearing my red dress with my red hood as I didn't have time to change it, which I now regret as I remember the small rips in it but also the very obvious color amongst the white snow. You never know what you might encounter this deep into the forest. I've never gone this far. I've never even been this far away from my village.

I sneak peaks at Legion every now and then throughout our walk, every time I look, I see him looking straight only appearing focused on the journey ahead. I begin to wonder if I'm even wanted here. It seems like I'm air to him. I mean I might as well not be here with how invisible I appear to him. I don't know what I expect from him but I know that the uncertainty of it all has sparked immense discomfort within me. Before he'd hold me so I wouldn't run away but now it seems he couldn't care less if I did. Or maybe he knows I've got nowhere to run.

Five hours of nonstop walking passes as well as the silence between us and Legion looks over his shoulder to where I've begun to slack behind. Not because I'm physically tired but because placing that small distance between us makes it feel like I've got more privacy to myself, even if I know it's not the case.

"Are you tired?" He speaks up for the first time since we left.

I peak my head up surprised that I'm finally being spoken to, but still feeling my stubborn side weigh on me, I simply mumble, "I'm fine." Which is true, physically I'm fine, perks of having an unnatural amount of power, but mentally I am very close to shutting down. It's all a lot to take in and I dread the inevitable time it'll all finally dawn on me.

Just as the words leave my mouth I notice the forest coming to an end and instead we're greeted by large mountains.

I've seen mountains before from my village on days where it wasn't foggy, but never up-close. The sight is truly impressive and I have to fight the instinct to open my mouth. The mountains are covered in snow, just like everything else in the north, and they almost look like ice mountains as it's hard to see any rock at all.

"Good because we're going over." Legion says now looking dead ahead with his head and back turned to me.

Going over?!

My eyes widen and I stop in my tracks. "Going over? As in over the mountains!? Are we not going around?" I hurriedly respond in a stressed tone.

Legion continues to walk. "It would take too much time going around." His tone however is as cool as the weather.

I start stumbling forward in an attempt to walk while also bending my neck to look up. "We can't do that." I press further.

"And why is that?"

I catch up to his determined strides. "It's freezing temperatures up there not to mention the trip alone is beyond exhausting."

There's only so much a white wolf can take in her human form. I'm not a Goddess afterall.

"We'll shift once we reach the mountains." At his words I understand the problem. He doesn't know that I can't shift. Not that I physically can't but that I won't. But I'll never tell him that, so to him won't and can't might as well be one and the same.

"I can't shift!" I blurt out without much thought.

He stops walking. I quickly stop as well to not stumble into him. "What do you mean you cannot shift?" His brows furrows as he turns his head to me again.

I feel my heart pick up it's pace and I swallow a newly formed lump in my throat. I have to think of a lie. "I've never been able to shift." I lie as I look away, I can't look him in the eyes, every time I do I feel the pull in my heart from the invisible string seemingly attached to his.

His men still far ahead of us stop too. Though they stay with their back turned to give the illusion of privacy. "You mean to tell me, you do not know how to shift?" He speaks with disbelief dripping from his words.

The lump I just swallowed is replaced with a new and I simply nod, not feeling confident that my voice won't give up my lie.

He takes a step closer while scanning me, he tilts his head and again steps even closer until my entire vision is preoccupied by his frame. I keep my gaze down trying my hardest not to look at him. "How could you have dared to go that deep into a forest as a simple fragile human?"

Oh no! Now what do I say?

"I like to run in human form, it makes me feel more normal." I stutter. Not completely untrue, it is true that running makes me feel more normal, but the human form... not so much.

"Do you not know how dangerous that is?" He quickly shoots back at me. It seems his disbelief is overridden by his protective nature.

"I know." I finally look into his eyes. His eyes are already staring me down however. His eyes flick a bit back and forth between mine and he sighs. "We still have to go over, you'll just have to endure." And with that he steps out of my vicinity, again turning his back to me as if I'm not there.

He starts to walk again as if our conversation changed nothing, and I suppose it didn't. By this point I don't care to argue anymore, it seems nothing right now will change his mind so I follow. His men of course start walking again. Soon after we reach a path leading up to the mountains and they all start following it. I hesitate a bit but follow along as it's not that steep.

The walk starts becoming more and more exhausting after an hour or so. The natural path disappeared a while back and now we are just walking on icy and snowy terrain that's only becoming more steep with every step it seems. I stumble often almost falling over but notice that it's only me and a few of his men who's struggling, but not Legion and the guy with the reddish hair. They know this way.

It's clear they've traveled through before. Just how many times have they done something like this...

At some point they're all so far ahead of me that I simply sit down on a snow covered rock. I'm tired since we've been walking all day and it's starting to become dark. I wish that I could just shift so I could harness my wolfs energy but alas it would be a death sentence. I'm sure he'll have my head within seconds, or have me chased for the rest of my life.

As I sit there I wonder if they'll just forget about me. Maybe they'll continue their walk and perhaps I can make it safely back once they're far enough away. In my wolf form I'm sure I can find my way. The sun has already set and the darkness could do me good, I can stay hidden in it. But I don't get to enjoy the thought for long as I feel someone pick me up. Lost in my wishful daydream I completely missed someone sneaking up. Of course it is Legion and I let out a yelp as he throws me over his shoulder. "Hey stop!" I sequel out.

"Why." He starts walking. "I am helping you." His grip on me is strong to secure me in place.

"I can walk just fine myself!"

He huffs "clearly."

"I can! I was just talking a break." I tap his back forcefully with my palm as I speak.

Legion doesn't respond to my action however he just continues to walk. "It's not much further Willow." He sounds unbothered.

I try to wiggle my way out of his hold, but his grip is too secure. "What do you mean?" My vision is of course nothing but his back side and the ground so I can't really see where we are.

"We're setting up camp for the night. My men have already made you a fire." He speaks nonchalantly.

"Put me down Legion." I sigh as I dangle over his shoulder.

Legion finally complies and my feet meet the ground. "We're here." He says and walks past me as if I'm air again.

Before me is a fire, his men had indeed been quick to make one, or perhaps I was slow. His men are nowhere to be seen however. "Where are your men?" I question.

Legion walks around the fire. "They're further ahead." It seems as if he's about to walk away as well and I start feeling a nervousness creep up inside me.

I follow along. "And where are you going?" I question timidly. I don't want him to sense my nerves but being left alone in the dark in an unknown mountain isn't exactly at the top of my list. My previous plan to flee home has been replaced by the fear of being alone. I've always been alone in spirit but being fully alone is new.

"I'm going to shift for the night." He doesn't stop walking.

"And what about me?" I speak louder feeling slightly out of place.

"Fire." Is all he says as he walks off into the dark.

My feet give up and stop moving after him as I sense it is useless. Instead I turn to the fire they've made for me. The light illuminates myself and the ground near but past the boarder of the light is a dark void. It unsettles me, and for the first time since we left I feel genuinely alone. With no chance to go home and an unwillingness to leave the comfort of the light, I'm alone.

I sigh and sit down closely by it. The fire warms my body and it dawns on me just how cold I've been. It doesn't take long for the cold weather to catch up on me however and I start shivering. I hug my legs closely in an attempt to help the fire warm my body. Thoughts of shifting start entering my mind and although it is tempting I know I just can't.

My head rests on my knees and I close my eyes. I know I can't sleep but I can at least rest my eyes hoping it'll count for something. I don't know how much time passes as I sit there but I feel so helpless I want to cry.

Then I hear a huff besides me and I'm quick to jump up in a defensive stance. I visibly relax as I'm met with the sight of black shiny fur. Legion is in his wolf form. His wolf is huge up close and I take a step back feeling intimidated in his presence. He's larger than me, both my human and wolf form. He takes slow steps towards me as he stares me down. I hold my breath involuntary, waiting to see what might happen.

He looks incredibly majestic in his wolf form, not that I'd ever say that out loud, but it would be a lie if I said he didn't.

He comes to a halt a short distance away from me and lays down. His head is still peaked up and his eyes haven't left mine.

I am still shaking. It's partially because of the cold and partially because of the intimidating wolf before me. It's clear that he notices my shaking because he starts scanning my body. He huffs again and prompts his head down on the ground.

I feel icy and I'm sure my lips have gone blue by now. His eyes are still focussed on me as if telling me something. Then it dawns on me what he wants as he motions his head to the spot next to him.

He wants me to lay down next to him. I hesitate but then he does it again and I give in. I give in because I'm not foolish, I may be stubborn but I know I can't get through another moment of this cold. I slowly move towards him and he follows my every move.

The tension grows the closer I get but I comply with his wish anyways. Without hurry I lower myself down and kneel next to him. I'm not close enough to feel his warmth fully though it's already warmer then the fire, perhaps I feel this way because of the bond... Still displeased he huffs again and motions to his side.

My heart feels like it's about to leave my chest as I follow his command and move right up next to him, still careful not to touch him even if we're merely a hair strand apart. He closes the gap and I'm engulfed in his soft fur.

He closes his eyes and after some time I relax my muscles that had tensed up somewhere along the way. I don't like giving him the satisfaction of feeling like he's helping me, but after the long walk, the exhausting day and the biting frost my pride can wait. So I get a bit more comfortable and lay down. His heat and vicinity brings me a feeling of safety. One that I've never felt before. And soon enough my heart slows down and my vision fades to black.

_______________________________A/N

And so the journey has started!

If you're still enjoying the story please consider voting and maybe leave a comment or two:)

Next chapter will be ready soon. And here's a little spoiler for you, they'll warm up a bit to each other, pun intended.

Until next time, byeeee.

CHAPTER 5 - CLOTHES

We're back to walking again, this morning was tense as I was awoken by Legion moving the second the sun arose. Throughout the night I had apparently gotten quite comfortable and had snuggled up to Legion, this made me feel extremely embarrassed and the feeling has been sticking ever since.

They all shifted back to their human form and we quickly ate some sort of bread that I've never tasted before and berries. It was actually quite delicious despite being cold. The rest of the bread was packed away in a bag that I hadn't noticed until now, carried by one of the brunettes. My guess is that they had kept the bag up here in the mountains, hidden safely while they ventured down in the forest for whatever reason.

Then we started moving again immediately, guess there's no time to waste with the king.

Speaking off, Legion has been looking at me more today, unlike yesterday I don't feel like air, but today I wish I was. The night still lingers around...

"We have three days worth of travel left." Legions voice fills the silence.

He's looking at me and I look around confused. He's talking to me?

"Willow?" There's a tint of confusion in his voice.

"Yes?" I keep my head down.

"Did you hear me?" He speaks with assertiveness.

I nod. I still feel like if I'm betraying myself by simply speaking to him, even just addressing his existence.

He quickly he slows his pace until he is walking right beside me. I raise my gaze, meeting his intense stare. "Are you ill?"

He must assume the cold of night has gotten to me, which I think it would've had it not been for him...

"No I'm fine."

He squints his eyes as if trying to pierce through my exterior and peer directly into my head . "I can sense something is wrong."

What a genius. Something is wrong, it's that I'm not home!

I scoff and roll my eyes.

"Do not roll your eyes at me." His voice is stern.

I stay silent. I know I shouldn't push him. Still wanting to triumph in some way, I ignore him. I want to return his favour from yesterday and make him feel like air.

Instead, I shift my focus to the surroundings, scanning the area. The mountains that are usually dressed in snow appear to lack some coverage and for the first time I notice how the tree's natural brown color is displayed. My eyes dart around in awe and upon further investigation I spot a cluster of trees ahead, covered with vibrant green leaves. Feeling ecstatic and overwhelmed by the hidden beauty of nature beneath the snowy facade, I dismiss Legion and pick up my pace.

An insatiable curiosity compels me to delve deeper into the green landscape. The trials ahead have become less steep, granting me a sense of walking on a straight path. I have no sense of how far up or down we are, but one thing is certain: the further I walk, the more the warmth embraces me.

As I press forward to pass two of Legions men, who are still walking in the front, my progress is abruptly halted as the man with reddish hair steps in front of me, cutting off my path.

"Let her." Legion's authoritative voice commands.

By the command of Legion the reddish haired guy retreats from my line of sight.

I continue my walk in the same awe. Nothing and no one will stop my discoveries through this breathtaking landscape. The sheer magnificence of it all fuels my determination, propelling me forward.

The forest becomes denser, with thick clusters of trees and an abundance of greenery obstructing my path. It becomes increasingly challenging to proceed without being hindered by branches and other obstacles. Despite my determination to continue, something inside me makes my body pause. This extraordinary sight before me is unlike anything I have ever experienced. Throughout my life, I have known only the monotonous expanse of snow, but now, surrounded by vibrant colors, I find myself entranced.

Time seems to slip away as I stand there, caught between wanting to savor the moment and feeling the urge to move forward. Suddenly, I notice an arm reaching out in front of me. I turn my head and realize that Legion is behind me, his arm extended. Without saying a word, he places a gentle hand on my lower back softly urging me forward to guides me through the dense forest. With his other arm, he skillfully moves aside branches, creating a path for us to progress together.

We continue our journey in silence, steadfastly making our way forward until we finally emerge from the captivating embrace of the forest. At the new sight I'm unable to suppress a gasp of astonishment. "Woah!"

Before me is a beautiful lake, a lake unlike any I have ever encountered. Its waters shimmer in a captivating shade of blue, while green grass surrounds it. The sun is high in the sky as it radiates with brilliance, illuminating this perfect oasis nestled among the mountains.

As I stand there, it feels as if I have stepped into a different realm. A magnetic force pulls my legs toward the glistening lake, drawing me closer.

"Stand by." Legion commands his men from somewhere behind me, but my attention remains fixed on the lake. Step by step, I make my way toward its edge, driven by my curiosity.

Upon reaching the water's edge, I lower myself down and find a comfortable spot. Taking off my shoes, I extend my feet toward the inviting water, dipping them into the cool, refreshing embrace of the lake.

As I cautiously dip my feet into the water, a delightful sensation overtakes me. The water is almost lukewarm, yet undeniably refreshing. Behind me, Legion approaches once again, although he remains standing.

"Have you ever seen a place void of snow?" He doesn't sound so serious anymore, his voice is more gentle now.

I shake my head in response.

"Quite a sight isn't it?"

I simply nod, completely mesmerized by the blue water before me. Its crystal-clear clarity allows me to see the lake's bottom, where small fish of various colors gracefully swim.

I sense Legion taking a step closer and I instinctively turn to face him, only to notice that he is shirtless now. My cheeks flush with embarrassment and I quickly avert my eyes. When did he take it off?

As I look away, I hear the faint sound of fabric rustling and I deduce that he is now removing more clothes, likely his pants. Does this man have no shame or regard for modesty?

I quickly avert my eyes, turning my head sharply in the opposite direction, wanting to avoid any possible glance at Legion's undressed state. In the midst of my embarrassment I'm interrupted by the distinct sound of a small splash. I swiftly spin my head back towards the lake, curious to discover the source of the sound. And there, to my surprise, is Legion swimming in the water.

Suddenly the undressing makes a lot more sense and I realize that the splashing shouldn't have been a surprise to me. I mean why else would he have undressed in the middle of a forest. Now with my gaze turned to him, I remind myself to exercise restraint, so I don't scan more of his body, even if part of me kind of wants to...

Behave Willow!

"The water is nice." He stares deeply into my eyes. They look almost as inviting as the lake.

Unable to tear my eyes away from his captivating stare, I watch as he effortlessly swims closer, until he's right beside my legs. "Join me." He sounds compelling, and I don't know if it's him or the lake but I almost dive headfirst into the water.

"But my clothes..." I stammer. I don't even know why I'm considering it but the lake just looks so refreshing and now with Legion in it a bigger force is pulling me in.

His eyes darken with something I can't put my finger on, at the mention of my clothes. I can't tell what it is but I'm certain that It's not anger... I've seen Legion angered far too much already.

He places his hands on my waist and I strangely enough don't object. My skin tingles under his hands and it spreads to the rest of my body making me feel slightly giddy.

What is this? First the night and now this. He must have me in a trance!

Gradually, I feel myself being lifted off the ground, as Legion scans my face as if waiting for me to object. However, words fail to materialize on my lips, leaving me utterly speechless. In this moment, my attention is consumed by the electrifying sensation ignited by the touch of his hands, keeping me captivated and unable to voice any resistance.

As there's no objection from me he slowly lowers me into the water. "Your clothes will dry in the sun." He announces before he he releases me, allowing me to submerge into the water and a satisfied expression flickers across his face, as if happy with getting his way.

I nod.

Wait why am I agreeing with this man?

Now without his hands on me the tingling diminishes and it becomes clear that my plan to ignore him isn't working. Determined to preserve some sort of loyalty to myself I propel myself away from him, hoping that the distance between us can act as a wake-up call for me.

Once I have placed enough distance between us I pivot my body to face him.

Much to my annoyance he has a smirk on his face as his eyes challenge mine. "You can pretend you don't want me all you want Willow but that's all you can do-" he swims closer. "-pretend." He finishes his sentence his voice laced with undeniable confidence.

Frustration bubbles within me. "Without the bond you'd be nothing to me."

He laughs. "The bond is what makes us meant to be so there's no 'without', as it is us who belong together because of it, you cannot change that."

I grow more frustrated. He's right, I know it but I don't want to admit it.

"Besides I'd still be your king." He looks smug.

An overwhelming desire to wipe that smugness off his face washes over me. Yet, opting for a more mischievous approach, I swiftly decide on the next best thing—I gather a handful of water and splash it in his direction.

As the water meets his face, he instinctively shuts his eyes, shielding himself from the sudden intrusion. When he reopens them his expression turns confused, replacing his prior smugness. It's a miracle that there's no trace of anger in his expression and an involuntary giggle leaves me as I see his face, unable to contain my amusement.

In a swift motion, he darts towards me, closing the distance between us. "You shouldn't have done that," he declares, his voice void of anger and instead ridden with playful undertones.

I shriek and try to frantically out-swim him however his previous quickness helps him gain a head-start on me and he catches me before I can even turn, leaving me no chance to escape his grasp.

With a firm grip, he pulls me close against his body. He holds me tightly against him ensuring there's no room for escape and with me being out of options and not wanting to feel more strange tingles I make another attempt to splash water in his face. I laugh as the water connects with his face and he squeezes me tighter so even my arms can't move. My breath hitches in my throat.

"Hey let me go." This feels familiar... but my voice sounds weak this time... out of breath.

"Will you stop splashing water on me?" His breath is still there some-how. How unfair.

I giggle again remembering his confused look. "Maybe."

He must've taken note of my everlasting mischievous tone as he responds. "Not good enough." His hands swiftly take hold of my hips, sending a jolt of seriousness coursing through me in an instant.

I suddenly realize how I'm pressed against Legion who's wearing nothing but his undergarments.

The tingly feeling intensifies while it spreads through my body igniting every nerve. Heat rushes to my cheeks, staining them with a vivid shade of red, as he adjusts our positions, aligning me more closely with him so we're more levelled. My body seems to have a mind of its own as it wraps my legs around him, entwining our bodies, against my will.

I feel him tense up as he inhales swiftly. I too tense up but my inability to breathe remains the same.

With his legs firmly grounded on the lake's bottom, he effortlessly guides us towards the edge. I feel a small hint of disappointment rise inside me, fearing that our moment is about to be cut short, however, much to my surprise, it's not. Instead of lifting me out of the water as I had initially presumed, he presses me against the edge, colliding our bodies together.

My heart picks up its pace, beating so fast it feels as if it's about to jump out of my chest. The same darkness from before washes over Legions eyes and he leans his head slightly closer to mine.

I wonder if he can sense my heart or my inability to breathe.

My body is still fully betraying me and I don't leave nor do I even try, instead I bite my bottom lip.

This catches Legions attention and his eyes moves to observe my lips. His hands squeeze my hips tighter and in response I close my eyes in a moment of elation.

Stop it body!

When I open my eyes again I've moved closer to him, or maybe he has? I don't know. All I know is that our faces are so close that I just have to lean in a little bit and our lips might touch...

"We must keep moving, my king!" One of his men interjects with a rushed tone, shattering the fleeting moment we shared. I feel my face burn as I realize that whoever called might've witnessed us like this. Legion releases his hold on me in a second though seeming rather unfazed as he exits the water and leaves me behind in the lake.

Well that plan definitely failed.

_______________________________________A/N

And the tension resumes...

Hope you liked chapter 5!

What do you think of the story so far?

As always don't forget to vote and I'd love a comment from you<3

chapter 6 - creature

L egion, his men and I left the lake behind, continuing our journey to his kingdom after the sudden urgency to leave, which still has me confused.

The naked landscape has turned into the familiar snowy terrain that I'm so used to again, but thankfully not before the sun dried me. As I trudge through the deep snow, the tension between Legion and me is palpable. Legion is more serious than ever, a different type of serious than I've seen before, and I am too embarrassed to speak yet again. We walk in silence for hours, the only sound being the crunching of snow under our feet.

A mix of emotions have been stirring within me for some hours now, anger at myself for letting my body react the way it did, fear of the unknown, and an attraction to Legion that still seems to linger.

Legion is the man who uprooted my life and forced me on this journey yet part of me is still happy that I went with him, a part that I wish to suffocate. I comfort myself however with the fact that it is most likely exclusively due to the bond playing tricks with my body.

He is so stubborn and so frustratingly confident in his actions, it is infuriating. And yet, there is something about him that intrigues me. Something that makes my heart race when I catch a glimpse of his stoney features, or feel his warm hand on my lower back. But again, I blame the bond.

Legion has seemed on edge ever since the lake, glancing over his shoulder every now and then as if he senses something behind us. His abnormal behavior also has me on edge and I can't help but to look over my shoulder as well. Whenever I look around though I can't see anything out of the ordinary, but the hairs on the back of my neck stand up regardless, and a chill runs down my spine as if something is in fact wrong, yet nothing appears to be. Perhaps Legions behavior has tainted mine beyond control.

Legion is staying painfully close to me while walking for the first time since we left my village, not letting me fall behind a single time despite my efforts. As we walk, Legion's broad shoulders brush against mine, sending shivers through my body. I try to ignore the sensations, but I understand now that I can't help the way my body responds to him, especially since the lake.

"Do you feel it?" he asks, his voice low.

"Feel what?" I wonder if he also feels the shivers as our bodies brush.

"Danger."

At his words I remember the hairs on my neck and ignore my attraction to Legion. I look around again, still seeing nothing, but I can't shake the feeling of being watched and Legion's close proximity isn't helping as it only makes my heart race faster.

"Yes." I respond feeling a sense of panic rise in me.

"Stay close." Legion replies.

My heart is racing and my palms are sweating. I don't know what this so called danger is, but I know it isn't anything I want to get familiar with, particularly because of Legions behavior.

We continue walking, faster now, his men alert, two in front and two behind.

My mind is a whirlwind of conflicting thoughts and emotions. The sense of danger is rushing in my blood and the sensation makes me want to shift as to protect myself, I know I'm strong enough for most danger. And also the feeling of wanting Legions protection but not wanting anything to do with him at the same time.

I can feel the weight of the imminent danger imposing on us with each step I take. Every instinct in me screams to be cautious, to remain vigilant, but my eyes betray me. They wander, against my will, towards him- Legion.

He stands there, with a sharp and attentive gaze, as if he can sense the danger lurking in every shadow. I should also check the shadows, yet I find myself unable to tear my eyes away from him.

Slowly, my gaze begins to trace the contours of his face, taking in every detail. His chiseled jawline, strong yet refined, commands attention. The subtle wave of his dark locks cascades over his forehead, framing his piercing eyes. Those eyes, like pools of liquid silver, seem to hold a thousand secrets within their depths. I feel there's much I've yet to learn, much I want to learn.

As my scrutiny intensifies, I become acutely aware of his flawlessly sculpted features. A strong nose that complements his dominant charm, lips that beckon with a hint of mystery. Even the play of light and shadow seems to conspire to highlight his striking countenance and features making him appear celestial.

But it is not just his physical appearance that captivates me. There is something beyond the surface, an unspoken allure that permeates the air around him. It draws me in, like a moth to a flame, despite the danger that looms. I know I should resist, should focus on survival, yet my gaze lingers, unable to look away.

Suddenly a flash of movement catches my eye. It is too fast for me to make out what it is, but it's enough to make me feel on edge. Legion must have seen it too, because he visibly tenses up and wraps his arm around me.

"What was that?" My voice is shaky.

Legion simply shakes his head and keeps walking. He then speaks in a foreign language to his men and they all seem to respond by tensing up.

Suddenly, the movement can be seen again. It goes by as fast as lightning, almost right in front of me and Legion. It's too quick for me to see what it is, but I can feel the gust of wind it leaves in its wake. Legions arm around me pulls me closer to him, and I know he saw and felt it too. Whatever it was it came too close to us.

Legion speaks again in the language I can't understand, I want to ask what he's saying but given the previous shaking of his head I doubt I'll get much out of it. I know whatever this is, it's a threat to us and I hate being left in the dark. Yet again Legions stubbornness could have me bubbling with anger if it wasn't for my fear right now. A part of me wants to blindly trust him.

I'm not used to being scared. Being a white wolf I always kind of thought I could take on anything, maybe because people around me always made me feel like white wolfs were savage monsters. But now that I'm out of the comfort of everything that's ever been familiar to me, I'm experiencing all sorts of things I've never felt or seen before.

Legion finishes saying whatever he was saying to them and they all drop their bags and leap into their wolf form within a second all around us, still with two in the front and two in the back.

Snarls and growls can be heard all around us from his men and just as I'm about to understand the real danger of the situation Legion speaks. "Don't be frightened, but do not say another word." His voice is practically a whisper.

I open my mouth to speak but his big hand covers my mouth before I can get a word out. "Don't." Legions voice is rushed.

I stare up at him in shock, confused and frightened at the same time.

Legions eyes are intense and I can feel heat radiating off his body. "We need to keep moving."

I simply nod now feeling like all I can do is follow his lead as this seems to be life or death.

Suddenly, one of Legions wolves lunges forward and bite down on the unknown creature in a blink and disappear into the snowy trees with the thing that had been moving too fast for me to see. Did it try to attack?

We all stand perfectly still as we try to watch the struggle in the trees, though the snowy terrain is covering them fully. Sounds of growls and aggressive snaps can be heard, then a sickening crunch emerges from the trees.

My heart drops... is the wolf okay?

I want to scream but any sound coming from my mouth is still muffled by Legions hand.

Legion leans down and whispers. "I trust you to stay silent." His hand lets go of my mouth and I try my hardest to keep my mouth closed as to not let a single sound escape.

He steps in front of me in a protective stance and covers me with his frame from whatever might exit the trees. A deafening silence has filled the mountain and all of the wolves stop snarling and growling. We're all just waiting. Waiting for the worst, but hoping for the best. As much as I dislike Legion and all his men I do wish that the wolf is okay and that the sound did not come from him.

I peak from behind Legion and squint my eyes hoping to catch a glimpse of something that can reveal what's happening.

That's when I spot something coming out from the trees and both me and Legion inhale in suspense. Thankfully it is Legions man still as a wolf, as he comes closer I notice a halt as if his front leg is injured slightly. I scan the rest of the wolf still on edge, he looks fine outside of the front leg, there is one odd thing though. His mouth is dripping with a white liquid that looks like it's almost glowing. His teeth are are drenched in the liquid and small drops of it hits the white snow as he walks towards us. Even though the snow is white I can clearly tell the liquid and the snow apart due to the glowing look the liquid possesses.

Legion breaks the silence. He speaks in the language that I don't understand and the wolf nods. He turns around to me. "It's okay now."

"What was that?" I ask, feeling just as scared as before.

Legion puts a hand on my shoulder and pulls me closer to him. "Nothing to worry about," he says in a softer voice.

"But what was it?" I insist.

"Just a wild animal," he replies dismissively. "We need to keep moving though." He turns around again. "Finley shift back and get dressed, the rest of you stay alert."

I don't know if he meant to say that in our shared language but it feels nice finally being able to understand him even if it is alarming to hear.

I look at him skeptically but don't argue. The three wolves remain in their positions around us and Finley joins them after he comes back in his human from the privacy of the trees. Two in front, one being Finley as a human and two behind, and we continue on our journey through the snowy gloomy mountain. Finley as I've now come to know him, doesn't appear very hurt, he must be a good fighter because that thing didn't seem weak. Far from it...

Despite Legion's reassurance, I can't shake the feeling that something is off. The way the wolves had reacted, the fluid dripping from Finleys mouth glowing in the snow... it all felt too ominous to be just a wild animal.

We stop to take a break eventually, and Legion leans against a nearby tree. I sit down in the snow in front of it, feeling his eyes on me.

"Are you okay?" he asks still very attentive as he's been since the lake.

I nod, unable to meet his gaze. If I look at him my eyes may reveal my lie that I am in fact not okay.

"Willow," he says more gently. "Look at me."

At that I can't help but lift my eyes to meet his, and in that moment, I sense a sincerity in his question. Perhaps he cares for me as more than just his possession... his mate.

Perhaps he even cares for me as an individual being. Or maybe he just wants to make sure his mate isn't broken beyond repair and isn't too frightened to speak, he does need to communicate with his plaything somehow afterall.

The tension between us is undeniable, and I wonder what is going on in that head of his. But then, the moment is broken as Legion's attention turns back to our surroundings.

He leaves the tree and wanders off to Finley. I watch him in silence as I place my head on my knees and hug my legs. I know I can't turn back now, and haven't been able to for a while, but sitting here alone with my own thoughts and confusion I wish for nothing more than to be back in my village with my mother.

Legion is just as hard to figure out as what just happened. I can never figure out what he's thinking.

Legion also won't reveal what the danger is, but I sense it is something to be wary off through his behavior, even now he acts as if the danger is still present. I don't know what was following us, and perhaps still is but I know that it is dangerous.

_______________________________A/N

A bit of a suspenseful chapter but I hoped you enjoyed it nonetheless<3

Hope you're still liking the story, and await the next chapters:) And if you've made it this far you could consider following me, it would mean a lot with the support.

Don't forget to vote or leave a comment. I love to read them and love to see my story being enjoyed by others!

Chapter 7 - Delirium

I can't sleep. Despite my exhaustion, my mind is racing with thoughts of the strange creature and Legion's silence. I lay next to Legions wolf form again. After a full day of walking while being on edge we sat up camp, with someone keeping watch at all time of course. Then we ate and immediately after got into our sleeping spots.

Laying next to Legion is just as nerve wrecking as the first time, but there wasn't much time to think about it this time as he had just walked up to me and laid down right by me and the fire. I think newer events might've made him even more stubborn than usual, perhaps one could call it protective.

However even Legions huge wolf form can't fully reassure me to sleep through the night despite how big he is, and I bet it's not helping that my heart acts out of the ordinary almost every time we touch and now my body refuses to sleep at all, even though I know I'll regret it in the morning. Traitor body. I toss and turn though in a gentle way as to not wake Legion, last thing I'd want is for him is to wake up and disturb me even more. I have contemplated letting his warm fur fully swallow me but I'm far too stubborn to even move an inch further.

I give up on sleep and open my eyes, having them closed while not even sleeping just seems like my body is mocking me. Instead my eyes find the reddish haired man- Finley. He is the one who's keeping watch for now until someone else taps him out and I can't help but feel a curiosity rise within me. This was the man that fought the creature. Who hurt it. If Legion won't give me answers then perhaps the man who saw the creature up-close will.

I get up and Legions wolf stirs a bit as if troubled immediately by the lack of my presence and I wait a few moments before I turn to approach Finley with a newfound determination, though while trying to be as quiet as possible so as not to wake anyone else, especially not Legion. "Hello," I say softly.

Finley doesn't move as he responds. "You should be sleeping." It's clear to me that he heard me approaching from far away.

I hesitate feeling slightly discouraged by his curt response, not sure if I should ask him anything anymore. But with my desperation for some answers I push through my inner desire to just turn around again and instead I sit down next to him by the fire.

"I can't sleep," I admit , "I keep thinking about that creature and Legion isn't saying much."

Finley nods seeming understanding for the first time. "Yeah, Legion can be a bit cryptic at times. But you have to trust that he knows what he's doing." His eyes have still not met mine, instead he's staring ahead into the fire.

I sigh, "I know that whatever that thing is, it is dangerous and I deserve to know more, since he was the one to drag me on this journey."

Finley looks at me for the first time tonight, his eyes brown and full of something I can't place my finger on. Closest thing I could say would be melancholy. "Talk to Legion about this."

I shake my head, "I have tried, but he won't tell me anything. I do not get him or why he insist on being the most infuriating man to have ever existed."

Finley looks down at his hands, appearing lost in thought for a moment. Then he looks back up at me and speaks, "be patient, Legion has been through a lot."

"What do you mean?" I feel an urgent need to know more.

Finley hesitates, as if debating whether to say more but then speaks after some time. "Legion's father was... quite hard on him. He always wanted more and expected a lot from him because of the title he had to pass onto him some day." He rubs his head with his hands. "His father was a very brutal man."

A pang of sympathy shoots through my body and my heart feels heavier than it should. I shouldn't care about this... but part of me does, a big part at that.

Finley continues. "His father was a cold man even to his own son. You can't blame him for speaking a language that was taught to him."

He raises his gaze to me once more. "He's always trying to do the right thing, even if it means keeping things to himself."

I look over at Legion's sleeping form, wondering about what type of stuff he might have endured growing up.A mix of sadness and inquisitiveness for him ascents in me.

"You have a good heart. And that's something that's hard to come by these days, so give him a chance to show you that he also has one, it's just hidden behind his hard exterior."

We sit in silence for a bit, both os us staring into the fire. I'm not sure what to respond to that so I simply don't. Not knowing how to proceed I switch subjects instead. "I'm guessing you won't tell me what that creature was then?"

Finley snorts letting out something close to a laugh. "No-"

Before he can say another word we're interrupted by a crunch behind us, we both turn around in a hurry to see Legion's piercing silver eyes staring back at us. How long has he been listening to us? And when has he shifted back?

"Is there something you would like to share with me?" Legion says, his voice as cold as the air around us. I open my mouth to answer but nothing comes out. Legion's eyes narrow, I can sense the tension in his body with his shoulders squared and his jaw clenched.

Finley and I look at each other, both of us with guilty expressions plastered on our face. I take a deep breath, preparing to explain myself, but before I can turn to say anything, Legion spins around without saying a word and walks away, leaving me with a sinking feeling in my chest while I watch his retreating form.

I cast a final glance at Finley, feeling embarrassed and ashamed for being caught. "I'm sorry, I didn't mean to cause trouble."

Finley nods sympathetically. "It's okay," he says. "Legion can be intimidating at times."

Reluctantly I move to return to my sleeping spot, the place where I had warmth in Legion's presence. With hesitant steps, I make my way back through the darkness, a faint disappointment tugging at my heart. I should just be happy that I annoyed Legion but for some reason I'm not. Maybe because he didn't seem annoyed, he seemed more... hurt?

As I approach the spot where Legion had kept me warm in his wolf form, a cold realization settles upon me. Legion is nowhere to be found. The comforting bulk of his body is absent, leaving behind an empty spot. It feels as though the night itself has grown colder, its chill seeping into my bones warning my night ahead. Something besides disappointment tucks at my heart and I wonder if Legion can feel the same through the bond, perhaps it is a shared feeling.

I search the dark with my eyes hoping to catch a glimpse of Legion silhouette but find none. His absence is like a silent message about his displeasure in me and suddenly I feel punished for my curious behaviour.

The moon's gentle glow casts an ethereal light upon the landscape, casting elongated shadows that dance in the cool night breeze. The silence is both eerie and deafening, amplifying the weight of Legion's absence. I peer around to remind myself that I'm not fully alone, the figures of sleeping wolves, the fire and Finley are still here at least.

A shiver courses through me, not solely from the cold, but from the lack of Legion. The more time that passes the more my mind has time to tell me stories of the creature and I grow nervous. Nervous that it will pay me a visit or maybe even Legion wherever he is. I wrap my arms around myself and decide to try and lay down, standing here won't do me any good, creature or no creature, our travels tomorrow will still be awful if I do not get any sleep to energize myself with.

•~•~•~•~•~•~•~•~•~•

I fail to sleep instantly despite my hopes to quickly sleep the night away. At some point during my efforts to force my body asleep Legion reappears and I immediately feel wishful that he might put his displeasure aside and lay down next to me again as I long for his warmth, but he doesn't seem to acknowledge me at all.

I glance up at him and my voice cracks as I try to speak "Legion, I..." I sit up. "I didn't mean to upset you. I just wanted to understand, to know what we're facing."

He meets my eyes but he doesn't say anything as he continues to walk.

The disappointment is evident on my face as Legion walks away completely disregarding my presence. I'm not sure where the disappointments comes from but I don't like it. He also seems to be better at ignoring my existence than I am at ignoring his. Perhaps that's the cause of my disappointment. Regardless I watch as the stoic man leaves me behind and instead approaches Finley. I cringe internally knowing that I might've gotten Finley in trouble.

Legion taps Finley on the shoulder, silently signalling for him to get up. Finley complies with a gentle demeanour, a demeanour Legion doesn't seem to reciprocate. He takes his place, standing guard, surveying our surroundings and Finley moves to leave shortly after without speaking a word, his gaze briefly connects with mine from the distance and I can't help but notice the weariness etched into his face before he disappears into the dark.

As I lie there, bundled up against the cold, I watch Legion's silhouette against the backdrop of the starry sky. I can't help but desperately miss the warmth his body provided and the comfort he brought that I didn't even realize, a comfort I especially could use tonight after our little encounter. But not because I like him I just want the extra guarding...

I wonder what thoughts occupy his mind. Is he disappointed in me or maybe starting to hate me, if he doesn't already that is. If he wishes he had another mate he can happily return me tomorrow, I wouldn't mind that! It's not like I want him anyways.

As he stands there attentive and stony, my eyelids start to feel heavier with every blink and the world around me blurs. I feel myself sinking further into a state of tranquility. The cool ground beneath me offers little comfort, but my weariness overrides any discomfort. Thoughts and worries of my safety gradually dissolve, replaced by a hazy dream-scape.

Every time I gather the strength to open my eyes I notice Legion standing in the same guarded manner as if he hasn't moved at all. Perhaps this man truly is made of stone. I chuckle to myself as my lids fall shut again.

Hours pass as the freezing cold seeps into my bones, I struggle to keep warm and fatigue begins to take its toll. I drift into a feverish haze, caught between wakefulness and dreams. Shadows dance on the edge of my consciousness, blending reality with illusions. Flashes of memories intertwine with imagined scenarios, creating a surreal tapestry in my mind.

Aaron's somber expression makes an appearance in the confines of my mind, a haunting apparition that weakens my heart. Desperate to escape the impact of his expression, I instinctively roll over, seeking refuge from the lingering image. But the respite is fleeting as another vision swiftly takes its place.

In this image, my mother emerges, her eyes brimming with tears. The sight tugs at my core, compelling me to reach out and gently brush her tears away. I want to assure her that everything will be alright, but before a single word escapes my lips, a chilling disruption shatters the silence. A wolf with fur as white as freshly fallen snow, strikes with ruthless precision, its teeth mercilessly tearing open my mother's throat. I cry out in a heart wrenching scream as I fall to my knees. Through the veil of my tear-filled, blurred vision, a figure emerges in the distance. As my horror-filled screams fill the air, my heart quickens at the sight of the man moving closer. My heart stops beating as I observe a disconcerting sight: a sinister smile forming at his mouth, accompanied by an eerie white liquid seeping out of his teeth.

The man etches closer and I hold my breath in anticipation causing my screams to end. A crack in my haze replaces the man with Legion, his face filled with what I assume to be worry. He blurs away as quick as he appeared, and an older man takes his place. The man is bearing an imposing crown, its presence commanding unwavering attention and my breath catches in my throat. In a moment of realization, a profound gasp escapes my lips, as the truth crystallizes before me. This figure, standing before me is none other than King Octavius himself. In his hand he holds something that makes my stomach turn: a decapitated white wolf head.

I turn to run but something grabs my shoulder keeping me in place and I cry out in anguish as I squeeze my eyes shut. It dawns on me that I can't shut them further and at that precise moment, a voice resounds, piercing through the shroud of fear.

"You're safe Willow."

Despite my fear to face the many horrors I've been introduced to tonight, something about the voice draws me in compelling me to open my eyes at once. I'm met with the same expression Legion had in my feverish stage merely minutes ago and without a moment's hesitation, I leap into his arms. Even though Legion is in a crouched position, he stands unwavering, unaffected by my sudden weight. A sharp inhale escapes his lips, and then, with an encompassing warmth, he locks me in a firm and secure embrace, erasing any trace of hesitancy in his initially uncertain arm placement on my shoulder.

"You're safe." He squeezes me tighter as I whimper in his arms.

_______________________________________A/N

I've had so many fever dreams it's not even funny and it always happens the worst places, have you guys ever tried anything like that?

If you like the story I'd really appreciate a vote on my chapters as it really helps to boost my story!

Until next time<3

CHAPTER 8 - BITTERSWEET ARRIVAL

It's the last day of our journey and I'm still slightly alert with every step I take. We have not seen more of the creature, or others for that sake, but an eerie unease still lingers and I often catch myself glimpsing over my shoulder or jumping at even the smallest sound. When I'm not on the lookout for creatures, I'm starting into the empty space. Today has been quite uneventful so far.

Surprisingly, the previous day seemed to pass by in a blur, unlike the others. Perhaps it's because I had gotten into the rhythm of things or maybe it was the newfound surge of energy I gained after the moment I shared with Legion during my night terrors. After the incident I could piece together that the awful imagery must have caused me to whimper out loud in my dreamy state and as Legion took notice of it, he came to my side. We still haven't talked about it, in fact we still don't talk much, however the silence hasn't been as frigid like it usually is. We share words every now and then, like when I need food or water, which is still more words than normally.

I wanted to say more yesterday or thank him or something, but the day ended before I could gain the courage. That night also passed by in a blink. As I fell asleep I felt at ease and I wasn't visited by more haunting imagery thankfully. I hadn't even fought the idea of laying next to Legion's wolf; I was, of course, hesitant as always, but the reality of things were that I was eager for the warmth and comfort he brought.

But there was one image that stuck with me, despite the lack of violence, like the other visions had possessed— the image of Aaron. My day yesterday had also been preoccupied by worries about him. I kept wondering how he was doing, if he was okay and if he even cares that I'm gone. Aaron isn't just any friend, he's my best friend and also the only friend I've ever truly had. And now one question hangs over me, will I ever see him again?

Back in the village I was somewhat of an outcast, which to be fair was probably my own doing. I had this fear of getting too close to people, knowing that it would only bring them one step closer to discovering my horrible curse. However, Aaron was relentless, he refused to let me off the hook so easily. He persisted until I finally realized that Aaron was the kindest soul to ever exists, and as we grew up together and he became a man, he still remained the kindest. Simply being near him was enough to cheer me up but now I might never see him again. I can't let that happen though, I refuse to die without having hugged Aaron again.

A weary sigh escapes my lips as I continue moving with the group, Legion and me still walking next to each other. His men are now all in their human form and although it means reduced protection I also find it somewhat comforting, as that must mean that there's less danger. We're also no longer moving up steep roads or straight ones, we are moving down and I can finally sense an end to this journey.

As if having read my thoughts Legion breaks the silence. "By the end of today, we shall arrive at my kingdom."

I keep my gaze fixed ahead, not bothering to meet his eyes, and continue my empty staring into the air at nothing in particular. "About time." I retort.

Legion chuckles lowly as if concealing his amusement from me. "And had we traveled around the mountains there would've been even more days left."

"But likely safer," I shoot back, my words carrying a hint of defiance.

"Perhaps, but less efficient." His voice is still tinted with some amusement.

I can't help but to roll my eyes. It's always about efficiency with this man.

"You know how I feel about your habit of rolling your eyes." Legion says, his voice now lacking amusement and instead coated with authority.

Suppressing the urge to roll my eyes again, I take a deep breath, recognizing the opportunity to use our conversation more productively. Perhaps I can even squeeze in a thank you, if I play my cards right.

I compose myself and try to dim my desire to annoy him further. "How long until we reach the kingdom?" I force the question out instead of a snarky remark.

"About 2 hours," Legion responds, his voice steady and unyielding.

"So soon!?" I fail to conceal my surprise, my eyes widening in disbelief as I turn to him checking to see if perhaps he misspoke.

"Yes," he replies, his gaze meeting mine without so much as blinking. A jolt of nervousness runs through me, mingled with a strange anticipation.

"What happens when we arrive?" I press on, my voice betraying a mix of curiosity and anticipation.

Legion takes a moment to scan my face before he responds. "You will be welcomed as the new queen, and we will follow our duties as mates," he states matter-of-factly.

"Follow our duties?" I repeat, my voice laced with a touch of uncertainty.

"Indeed. I shall mark you, and you shall mark me, and we shall-"

"No!" I interject abruptly and urgently, cutting his sentence short.

Legion's expression turns slightly puzzled as he waits for me to continue, however as I don't he resumes. "...have a ceremony."

"Oh..." I mutter feeling slightly embarrassed about my small outbreak. I avoid his eyes, desperately hoping that he doesn't piece together the reason behind my sudden and intense reaction.

Legion's strides are steady unlike mine, my legs have, contrary to his, started to become somewhat wobbly causing me to walk with the looming uncertainty that I might stumble if I'm not careful.

"I won't make you do anything against your will." His words make my stomach sink in a split second as I nervously wait for him to call me out.

"And definitely not what you thought I was going to say." Legion continues and I stumble making me fall behind. Embarrassed that he did understand the cause of my outburst I simply stay behind.

"Though it will happen," Legion asserts while keeping his own gaze straight ahead.

It takes me a moment to realize what his words mean but when I do, any embarrassment I could've had lingering is replaced with a fiery pride. "It won't," I retort defiantly, my voice surprisingly firm and resolute.

"With time, then," he counters not seeming fazed by my stern tone.

His reaction to my response only fuels my fire more. "NO," I say louder, my voice rising with conviction as I speed up my pace to match his.

Legions pace stays the same as it has been through our conversation, making him seem like a moving statue with no emotion. "Willow, you can't resist me. I can assure you, the longer you prohibit yourself the extends of the bond, the stronger the bond will become, and the harder it will be to resist me," His voice is carrying a mixture of certainty and challenge.

"The bond doesn't control me," I exclaim, trying to sound as disgusted as possible. I can't have him thinking I have some deep desire for anything he could possibly give me.

"I'm well aware of that by now. But I can sense that you want me in more ways than one." He returns his eyes to mine without a single doubt in his gaze and with a continued stony expression. Where does this man get his confidence from?

My stare flickers between his eyes scanning for any type of cracks in his confident exterior but I find none. "You're delusional, of course I don't!" The volume of my voice is enough to sense my frustration.

"If that's the truth, then why does your heart beat faster whenever I touch you?" Legion probes, his voice almost teasing.

"It's the bond," I quickly shoot back, attempting to deflect his observation. Does this mean he has noticed my heart all those times... Is he able create the tingles on purpose?

"The bond doesn't control how you feel about me, just that you're connected to me," Legion starts to explain. "If you feel a pull towards me, that's the bond ensuring we find each other. We're destined to be mates, after all. Unless you think The Moon Goddess makes mistakes of course. But if you feel your heart flutter whenever you're close to me, or your breath hitch in your throat, or even that frustration you have towards me, then that's all you."

I blink continuously as I try to find a counter argument, but as I find none I simply deny his claims. "Not true!"

He tilts his head in a smug manner. "Then how come you didn't reject me?" Legion challenges me.

"I tried-" I begin to explain, but he interrupts me.

"No, you acted irrationally once, in the heat of the moment. If you truly wanted to reject me, you could have done so since then on many occasions, but you haven't... ask yourself why," his words pierces me and I have a burning desire to silence him in whatever way possible.

"You wouldn't have let me," the volume I speak with has decreased rapidly and I sound almost defeated.

Legion narrows his eyes at me and I notice an anger combined an emotion I can't pinpoint wash over his eyes. "Alright then, I won't be a fool for someone who does not want me. If it's truly what you want, then go ahead, no one will stop you," he states firmly, his eyes staring into mine with a penetrating look so grand it almost feels like he has the ability to read every thought I've ever had.

Silence fills the air all around us, and I become painfully aware of his mens presence for the first time since the beginning of the conversation. I feel the weight of the countless stares upon me, awaiting my next action. My hands tremble and I fiddle with them as my eyes begin to sting with the choice I've been given.

I frantically look around, feeling small and exposed under their piercing looks. As my eyes jump from man to man, I notice how everyone looks expressionless except Finely, as my eyes land on him I sense a look of concern. If it wasn't for my slightly blurry vision I'd say he looked almost pleading. The hint of worry in Finleys expression only adds to my vulnerability as I stand there trying to decide what to do or say. I struggle to find my voice amidst the turmoil raging within me but I know I must say something if I want this to end.

"I..." I trail off, my voice barely a whisper.

Legion looks at me with narrowed eyes as he crosses his arms in a challenging manner, daring me to make a decision.

"I can't find my way back alone," I finally say nervously, trying to stall my inevitable decision.

Legion clenches his jaw before he replies. "I'll have Finley escort you, then. What will it be?" His tone is growing impatient.

As I stand there under their scrutinizing looks my pride and my heart engage in a fierce battle. My breath feels shaky as well as my hands and my head hangs low with a hope to shield myself a little from the many eyes, but in the end I know I need to act. I take a deep breath and close my eyes just as I feel more water gathering in them. As I stand there the embarrassing truth is clear to me; my weak heart wins. I open my eyes again but I drop my gaze fully to the ground in defeat as I walk past Legion without saying anything.

"Very well." He states his tone ruthlessly disregarding the state I'm in. He sounds like he never once questioned the final outcome, which he probably didn't given his endless source of obnoxious confidence.

•~•~•~•~•~•~•~•~•~•

We are still walking, the tension between us suffocating and the atmosphere thick with awkwardness. I feel a deep sense of humiliation and a knot in my stomach that won't go away. The many unspoken words hang heavily in the air.

As we walk I try to distract myself by thinking of happy times in my village, but almost every happy memory I have is naturally shared with Aaron, the only friend I have, and my mother. I try to think of something else but images of both of them keeps resurfacing in my mind making the knot in my stomach tighten even more.

After what feels like an eternity of unbearable silence, I gather the remnants of my shattered courage and speak up, my voice barely audible above the noise of our footsteps. "I do have a request, though..." I nervously peer up at Legion.

He swiftly looks at me out of the corners of his eyes and return his gaze ahead. "What is it?"

"I want to see my mother and Aaron again." My tone remains gentle and low, hoping that he will take my request serious.

"Certainly, you'll see your mother again."

The happiness of a small victory warms my body but before a smile can form on my lips I scrunch my eyebrows in confusion. "And Aaron." I state wishing that he simply misspoke.

"There's no need for you to see him again."

My mouth opens but no words come out initially and I try again. "What do you mean." I finally ask in disbelief.

"I meant what I said." Legion replies firmly leaving no room for objection.

I disregard his tone and object anyways. "He's my best friend!"

He tenses up at my words and clenches his jaw. "We can discuss that later." He declares as if he senses I won't back down from this.

Just as I'm about to argue with his statement he speaks up again. "We're here."

In an instant, I snap my head forward, and my eyes widen in disbelief as a colossal castle stands grand in the near distance, taking my breath away. I come to an abrupt halt, my feet rooted to the ground as I admire the castle in awe. I want to move closer but my feet are glued to the ground, it feels as if the weight of our long journey has culminated in this singular moment.

Sensing my hesitation, Legion comes to a stop as well, his presence ever watchful. He extends his hand, offering it to me as a gesture of support, but my focus remains fixed on the castle, unyielding. Ignoring his outstretched hand, I stride past it with determination, and Legion lets out a faint amused snort followed by a string of words in an unknown language directed at his men. They gracefully step aside, allowing me to proceed unhindered. I can sense Legion's presence trailing closely behind me, letting me lead the way.

Eagerly, I quicken my pace as we descend the remainder of the mountain, infused with newfound energy sparked by the sight of the kingdom. It doesn't take long before the kingdom is completely covered by the many trees we encounter on our way down and I'm quick to grow impatient. The journey down is marked by my silence, completely struck with anticipation as I await a sight of the kingdom again. Seeing the castle alone makes the entire journey seem worth it. Legion follows behind in reverent silence, allowing me to process the breathtaking sight that'd just unfolded before us.

With every step, the anticipation grows within me making the air seem almost electrifying. I finally see the forest edge and my steps speed up. I break through the many trees and my eyes immediately dart around taking in the colossal castle in the distance. It's huge stone walls rise impossibly high, reaching towards the heavens as if proclaiming its unrivaled power. Every block, weathered by time and history, adds to the imposing grandeur that radiates from its very core.

I lower my gaze slightly and also take note of the many surrounding villages part of his kingdom leading up to the huge castle walls. They're filled with people and life as they all go about their day, they've not yet spotted us and I feel an unease wash over me, how will they react to me?

Legion, must be understanding the impact this sight has on me, as he remains silent, letting me soak in the glory of his kingdom. I don't even need to turn around to know he has a proud look plastered across his face.

I slow my steps down as the sight overwhelms me. Suddenly it all dawns on me at once; this is my new home, my new kingdom. I almost turn around right then and there and sprint all the way back home. I take a timid step back, only to collide with something solid. Startled, I turn around to see what it was, and to my surprise, I find Legion standing right behind me. How had I not noticed his presence before? His gaze meets mine, and with only three simple words, he asks.

"Are you ready?"

_______________________________A/N

They arrived! Finally lol:)

Next chapter is already in the making~

As always I'd love your support, so leave a comment or vote it helps a lot!

If you're still reading you should follow me to keep track on updates or similar if you want.

Byesies for now<3

Chapter 9 - Unfamiliar Welcome

I'm not ready but I step forward nonetheless, my breath caught in my chest. I move slowly because I'm worried about getting spotted and and I sense Legion following behind me, seeming attentive to my every move. Nervous energy courses through me, making each step feel heavier than the last.

I'm walking ahead of everyone but right as we're about to trudge through the village I slow myself down quickly to allow Legion to pass me and hopefully walk in front of me in an attempt to go unnoticed, but instead of passing me like I had hoped, he simply walks besides me, not letting me fall behind.

"There's no hiding." He says in a low and controlled voice and I realize he's right. Some villagers have already begun to stop in their tracks upon noticing us.

As their eyes fall on Legion, their king, I witness an instant shift in their gaze. Respect and admiration fill their expressions, their faces illuminated with awe yet also a type of nervousness hides beneath the surface. It's a sight I've seen before, back in my own village when Legions presence became known. But this time, it feels different—more significant. As we pass by them they bow their head down low as a sign of respect.

Time seems to slow as the villagers' attention shifts towards me as well. Confusion and curiosity flicker in their eyes and they even pause their activities completely. It's as if the world around them has momentarily frozen, their focus solely on the stranger who stands beside their revered king.

A comforting touch brushes against my lower back, and I glance sideways to find Legion's hand resting there. The contact instantly calms me, providing a brief respite from the curious stares. Yet, the weight of their scrutiny remains a source to a newfound anxiety.

Looking around at the many speechless villagers, the realization sinks in—I am about to become the Luna and the queen of this kingdom. The thought alone is enough to make my heart quicken its pace, however something about that also doesn't feel real.

My eyes flicker around and I try to make myself seem smaller, though unsuccessfully. The villagers eyes are also flickering, they're switching between me and Legion. Some appear frozen, others in awe and there's even some who look almost horrified, and I start to wonder if perhaps it's because their king is touching some peasant girl.

I wouldn't call myself a peasant though, my mother and I lived well but compared to these people... they all look like they belong in a castle. Legions kingdom appears to be thriving which only makes all of this seem so much more intimidating. I'm truly an outsider.

I peer up at Legion to see if he is affected by the stares at all but he is simply looking straight ahead with determined eyes, not paying attention to them. The stony man is clearly used to it.

In a blink his gaze shifts and he peers back into my eyes and my breath hitches in my throat involuntary, he then gives me a reassuring nod and I avert my gaze. I can't take any more eyes at me or I fear I'll malfunction.

The villagers faces are all coated with different expression and they are all hard to read through my racing thoughts. However no matter how they look they all have one thing in common, they bow their head down when we pass. And some of the younger women in the village even courtesy while appearing slightly giggly.

They either love their king or they're really good at faking it...

The walk through the village seems never ending, it's so quiet that all I can hear is my heart, which is beating faster and harder than it should. The warmth of Legions hand is practically burning my back but also works as an anchor somehow, helping to steady me.

After what seems like forever we leave the village behind, and I take a deep breath that I hadn't realized I needed. My head feels like it's spinning and my vision is hazy.

All my life I've practiced going unnoticed and I became good at it. I doubt many people in my village even knew my name, so this is way more attention than I've ever had before, outside of when Legion paid a visit to my village, but back then I was more focused on trying process that I had a mate. Now though there's nothing to hide behind, this is really happening and there's no way for me to go unnoticed.

We set foot on a road that stretches endlessly towards the colossal castle, its distance now dawning on me as much greater than I had imagined. The path ahead appears daunting, almost unfathomable to travel in a single day, but Legion said we would arrive today so surely it can't be that far...

But as I study the road ahead more, another realization hits me, intensifying my bewilderment. It becomes clear that this road is the solitary path leading to the castle. There are no other paths, no alternative routes.

It hangs suspended like a fragile thread, a lifeline amidst the unknown. Its structure resembles a bridge, an enigmatic link between the villages and the castle. I peer slightly over the edge scared of what I might find but a mystical mist obscures what lies beneath.

The mist-covered abyss, lurking just beneath the road, adds to my confusion. Its depths are concealed, but I somehow know that it goes down further than I'd like. If I were to veer off the road, if I were to lose my footing and fall into the unknown, I have no idea of where I might find myself, but I do know it wouldn't be alive.

"How far down does that go?" I question with a shaky voice feeling the effects of the height settle into me.

"Very far." Legion simply says his hand now gripping onto my hip keeping me suspended next to him.

I find myself leaning against Legion without second thought. My pride can wait.

"Don't fall." He continues and Legions men chuckle slightly from behind us.

I don't know if it was an attempt at a joke or if he was serious, but either way I'll gladly take his advice.

Somewhere along the way I loose my sense of time that I suspect fear plays a part in. It feels like we've walked nonstop for hours, yet every second seem everlasting. I stay glued to Legions side as we venture the rest of the road.

•~•~•~•~•~•~•~•~•~•

At last we reach the castle! The walk had been silent and tense. I had simply focused on the castle ahead and my goal to reach it without falling to my death. Not that the road was small but the fact that it's above an endless abyss didn't exactly calm my nerves. But at last... the castle is right in front of me. Bigger than I ever could have imaged.

The castle stands tall, its stone walls a testament to its power. It commands attention and reverence, which I'll gladly give it. In fact my mouth might pop open at any moment if I'm not careful.

With a small push on my lower back from Legion, who has noticed my hesitation, I move. Legion and I approach the massive doors that guard the entrance to the castle. They stand before us, as a grand barrier yet to be crossed. They're beyond grand, in fact they're so colosal they seem to stretch on forever and I fail to find the top of them even with my head fully tilted upwards. I take a moment to steady my breathing and to process it all.

The doors possess intricately carved designs that depict all kinds of stories, my guess is the kingdoms stories of their glorious past. I marvel at the craftsmanship, the dedication and skill that has gone into every detail. These doors hold the weight of centuries, and soon they will open to welcome me into my new home. And again it doesn't feel real.

My shaky hand instinctively reach out to touch the stories that are crafted into the wood, perhaps as a reality check, but just as my fingertips brush the door it opens with a loud creak causing me to jolt backwards. Legion allows me to step behind him this time as we await for the doors to fully open.

It takes time for my eyes to adjust to the darker atmosphere in the castle but when they do my eyes widen in disbelief. The massive doors swing fully open and I notice hundreds of people standing in perfect formation on either side, their gazes fixed on us. A guard's commanding voice cuts through the air, declaring, "King Legion and his men have returned!"

The announcement seems unnecessary as everyone are already watching us however I quickly sense a shift in the air. Countless faces morph from a deep respect to confusion and it dawns on me that Legion has deliberately stepped aside, allowing them to discover my presence. I want to curse him out but alas I must try to keep myself level headed. Or at least portray myself as such in front of all these people.

However a surge of anxiety does make me to entertain the idea of running back across the bridge that I would never even have considered stepping a foot on seconds ago, but before I work out a plan to escape the hundred of eyes Legion speaks up with an assertive tone to break the silence.

"This is your new queen and Luna. You will give her the same respect you give me." He says it definitely, allowing no room for protest and they all nod their heads simultaneously as if they had rehearsed it. Although confusion lingers on their faces, they remain obedient, refusing to object or stray from their designated positions.

Legion's hand firmly finds my lower back again as he urges me forward, this time I'm more defiant but move nonetheless determined to maintain some semblance of control and composure in front of all these people.

We stride through the precise formation of lines, passing by individuals who I presume to be guards, servants and nobles. In a synchronized display of respect, they all kneel before us, bowing their heads in a profound show of respect. It feels surreal, as if I've stepped into a dream that could shatter with the blink of an eye. With every step I take I feel more lightheaded, and I make sure to keep my head down too scared to face anyone head on.

I doesn't take long for Legion to notice and tap under my chin, silently telling me to keep my head up, and I comply as well as I can. I try to keep my gaze ahead but my eyes betray me every now and then, as I glance at the people surrounding us. They look even more glamorous than the villagers, as if that was even possible and I feel even more out of place than I already did in my worn out dress.

After our walk down the long hall we reach some stairs leading upward, covered in a red carpet. Legion turns us around to face his people. As we turn around I notice that his four men hadn't followed behind us but instead disappeared, seemingly out of thin air. I scan the crowd an extra time for some reddish hair, seeking comfort in a, now, familiar face, but the man is nowhere to be seen.

As we stand there in the silence that blankets the hall, everyone awaits Legions next move. He takes a moment to peer over the crowd before he shoots everyone a firm nod and they all get up and break their previous perfect alignments.

Conversations start to spark, and the room comes alive with a renewed energy, yet the tension doesn't fully resolve as many curious stares pierce my way. Before I can worry too much about the murmurs that unmistakably revolve around me, Legion turns us to guide me up the grand staircase. I follow his move wordlessly, muted by the overwhelming greeting we had just received and the lasting stares on me.

Just as we begin our ascent, a voice interrupts our progress from behind. "Well, well, well," the voice playfully chimes. I glance over my shoulder, spotting a woman with sleek black hair. She continues, "Behold, my dear cousin returns, and he brings along a woman."

Her tone is lighthearted, aiming to alleviate the tension that hangs in the air. Legion adjust his body to face the woman and lets out a weary sigh in response.

The woman turns her gaze towards me with a mischievous glint in her eyes. "He departs with four and returns with five. A woman at that," she continues, her words tinged with humor. It's evident that she possesses a charm and wit that she wields effortlessly.

Her playful remark hints at the unconventional nature of our arrival, but there's no trace of malice in her voice however and I instantly feel somewhat relaxed in her presence. She glances at Legion, but he remains silent with an impassive stare.

The woman with black hair then redirects her attention to me again, her warm smile welcoming me. "Well, shall I assist you in settling into your new home? You must be exhausted from the journey."

Before I can respond, Legion speaks on my behalf. "You can show her to my room Marisa. I have duties to attend to," he declares, taking charge of the situation. His words don't go unnoticed by me though and I quickly feel a discomfort wash over me.

Refusing to accept his decision, I muster the courage to argue, "I don't want to stay in your room." I sound firm although my voice is still shaky and Legion's brows furrow in response. However, before he can counter my objection, the so called Marisa interjects.

"You know it's against tradition to share a room before the ceremony," she states, her tone turning more serious as she addresses Legion. She almost sounds like a mother scolding her child.

Legion pauses, his gaze shifting between Marisa and me, contemplating our words. After a brief moment of consideration, he relents. "Very well. She will have her own room," he sounds almost too tired to argue. My guess is that this Marisa lady has gotten in the way of his plans before and it makes me like her just a little more.

Relief floods through me. I won't have to share a room with this stubborn statue of a man. Although he's my mate, he's also a complete stranger and I still have some dignity left.

Turning her attention back to me, Marisa extends a hand. "Come, I will show you to your own room. You can rest and prepare for the upcoming ceremony," she says, her voice filled with reassurance.

Her voice is so melodic that I feel more at ease. Even the air around her seems lighter than the heavy air Legion carries. I shoot him a final look. Legion, as expected, doesn't show much emotion, but I do notice a difference in his eyes. They appear softer as he peers back at me. Softer than usual. Not having the energy nor brain power left to wonder what it could mean I turn back to Marisa.

I grab the her hand and we begin our ascend. Then Legions speaks up. "The ceremony will take place in two days. Prepare her."

With those words we continue our climb of the staircase together with a new pit of worry growing in my stomach.

•~•~•~•~•~•~•~•~•~•

Marisa guides me through the labyrinth-like halls of the castle, her confident steps echoing against the polished marble floors along with her cheery voice, and even though I don't hear a single word she says she continues to talk.

Eventually we arrive at my temporarily assigned room, and as the doors swing open I almost gasp. The room is beyond anything I've ever seen. Definitely fit for royalty and not someone like me. I'm urged forward by Marisa before I can think further and we step into the big room.

"This is your room, Your Highness. A place of relaxation and comfort within these strict castle walls." She shoots me wink and I attempt to smile. "Please just call me Willow." I state awkwardly.

Marisa ignores my words and instead walks me through the room's features, her voice matching that of the silk curtains.

When she's done she's almost out of breath, while I'm still trying to remember what she said about the pillows being made by some famous pillow person, or something like that.

She walks past me and sits on the nearby couch. "Well alright your Highness, any questions?"

I want to correct her again but I'm more distracted by the fact that my entire house back home could fit into this room more than just once, so I simply shake my head. I step further into the room, only now daring to move on my own.

My attention is drawn to the opulent canopy bed pressed to the middle of the wall to my right. With its plush pillows and intricately embroidered linens looking more comfortable than anything I've seen these past couple of days of traveling, or ever even. Perhaps this has caught my attention due to the many hours of walking and bad sleep.

Marisa notices my gaze and gestures towards it, a warm smile gracing her lips. "Your bed, fit for a queen. Rest assured, it will provide you with the utmost comfort during your time here."

It's clear that my tiredness has indeed caught up to me as her words are barely audible to me through the thought of diving headfirst into that bed.

Before I can do any such thing an unknown woman steps into the room. Marisa calls her forward. "Please, prepare a bath for Her Highness. Fill the tub with warm water and add some of those soothing oils."

I blink in disbelief. The woman is a maid?

She disappears quickly after nodding her head but soon reappears with oils and fresh flower petals before I've even had the chance to deny the request. Not wanting to be a bother I keep my mouth shut, simply studying my surroundings.

I also start daydreaming about sleeping as the maid hurries into, what I assume to be the bathroom to fulfill Marisa's request.

I stand around awkwardly while fidgeting with my hands. As I hear the bathtub being filled I glance at the bed wishing I could simply lay down right here right now.

Then while longing for sleep I catch a glimpse of movement in the corner of my eye but I'm too slow to see what it is. Marisa doesn't comment on it either. I do notice one thing though; my bag has magically found its way to the room, now sitting in the corner. Relief washes over me as I realize my belongings have just been delivered by someone.

These people sure move quick...

Marisa also notices my bag as she speaks. "You shouldn't worry about your old clothes. These closets are stocked with as much clothes as a heart could desire. I'm sure most will fit perfectly."

Some anxiety that I didn't even know I had dissolves as this means I'll have a bigger chance at blending in. My current outfits look nothing like Marisa's or the other women's in the castle.

I nod my head as a response and she sends me a smile.

As the maid completes the preparations for my bath, the room fills with the soft scent of flowers and warm steam. Marisa, sensing my need for privacy, excuses herself with a graceful yet teasing curtsy, leaving me alone to enjoy the water. Although I don't mind Marisa, I'm relived to be more alone.

With anticipation I make my way to the bathroom. It's covered in polished marble and glistening fixtures. The maid, with a respectful nod, gestures towards the awaiting tub, its edges adorned with rose petals. She also excuses herself leaving me to undress alone. Finally alone I think with a deep breath.

After I've undressed I ease into the warm water, letting its comforting embrace envelop me. The worries and anxieties of the day seem to melt away with each gentle ripple and I close my eyes, taking a long waited rest.

In this private sanctuary, I allow myself a moment of vulnerability. But even though I'm relaxed thoughts of the impending ceremony creep into my mind. It's the only thing keeping me from actually falling asleep.

Legion also make an appearance behind my eyelids. His stature, his black hair, his silver eyes. I try to get rid of him by opening my eyes but every time I close them again it seems he's burned his way into them. The bond still has me under its control and I sigh involuntary.

Sitting there in the warm water with Legions silver eyes watching me even when he's not around seems like a poor joke. Thankfully I gradually manage to drift further into relaxation, simply ignoring him and his intense eyes, almost feeling like I'm on the edge of falling asleep.

I decide to get out, knowing that I'll turn into a sleeping raisin if I stay much longer.

Feeling exposed but not wanting to wear my dirty clothes, I leave my worn-out dress on a counter and open the door to check if anyone else has devices to pay me a visit. When I see that this isn't the case I walk into the bedroom again to find something fresh to wear, and hopefully something that'll make me blend in more.

To my surprise I don't have to search far as a soft, silk robe has been thoughtfully laid upon the bed along with some a meal on a tray. The meal looks beyond appetizing and my mouth waters. I quickly wrap myself in the comfort of the robe, while preparing myself for the food I'll soon eat.

The fabric caresses my skin, as it sticks to my slightly wet form. I run my hands over the silk.

Where do they get this kind of material, it's softer than anything I've ever felt.

I grab some fruits from the tray to nibble on before I take a step towards the closet wanting to explore my other options and realize that my hair is still soaking wet, as the sensation of it dripping down my back makes me fully awareness of my own vulnerability. The air, slightly cool against my damp skin, makes me feel even more vulnerable.

As I stand in front of the wardrobe, a mix of excitement and self-consciousness fills me. I eagerly anticipate the opportunity to explore the treasures within, but at the same time, I become aware of my own lack of clothes. The robe, while offering some modesty, also exposes hints of my feminine form, revealing the curves and contours beneath. A silk robe only covers so much...

I begin to run my fingers through the rows of garments, my touch lingering on the delicate fabrics that are unlike any I've ever felt before. But in the midst of my exploration, a sudden sound shatters the moment.

A creak behind me makes my heart skip a beat. I turn in a hurry, my robe fluttering around me, only to find Legion silently framed in the doorway. His piercing gaze sweeps over me, and for an instant, time seems to stand still. His silver eyes are no longer just in my mind, they're really here staring at me.

The moment lingers a little too long and an electrical tension fills in the air. Its as if this electricity will zap me if I dare move, so I don't. His eyes seem to darken right before me and I wonder if I'm just imaging it or if a storm really is forming in his gaze.

The silence between us seems to stretch, amplifying the odd energy that lingers through the room.

Finally, breaking the spell, Legion's voice emerges, husky. "I see you've settled in. I shall leave you to relax for the day." His tone betrays his usual composure and I start feeling completely bare under his eyes. As if reading my thoughts he averts his gaze before I have a chance to think about covering myself in some way.

With Legions eyes now avoiding me like I was cursed a rush of conflicting emotions washes over me. Part of me wants to see more of that side of Legion. But another part wants to hide under the covers in the gigantic bed.

With a nod, I acknowledge his words, and he is gone in a blink as if it physically hurts him to stay.

As I stand there, the room now feels hollow compared to the previous filling presence of Legion. The robe that draped me in its silky embrace now seems more exposing than ever and I become painfully aware of just how much reveals.

I return my attention to the closet with a urgent purpose; finding some clothes quick. I can't seem to shake the electrical sensation that lingers in my room from our recent meeting.

Then I start to wonder... just how long had he been standing there?

———————————

chapter 10 - silent solace

Waking up in a bed for once since I left my village feels amazing, not to mention the bed in itself is softer than any bed I've ever felt and could probably fit a dozen people.

After the late visit from Legion no one else came to my room, I suppose they know the importance of alone time, but I bet many in the castle are dying to find out more about me and I doubt Legion is one to talk. He's a man of few words afterall.

I sit up in the bed undoubtably with messy hair. My hair is always a mess but the mornings are especially bad. My hair, much like myself is simply a mess. However at least my hair can be helped with combs and pins, I'm not really sure what to do about myself.

Being here still doesn't feel real and I quickly contemplate staying hidden in this room forever to avoid any of my new titles. Technically they became mine the second I felt a string tug at my heart when I met Legion, but knowing that there's a ceremony tomorrow makes me want to go back to sleep, but alas I cannot, which I'm reminded of as someone knocks at the door.

"Good morning Your Highness, did you sleep well?"

I recognize the voice of Marisa through the door and I stretch my arms out as I answer tiredly. "I slept better than I have in days."

She chuckles lightly and opens the door. "I bet." Her eyebrows lift as she takes in my sleepy state. "Still a sleepyhead I see."

I simply shrug in response. It was a long overdue sleep, nothing could make me feel bad about it.

She clasps her hands together. "Well up you go. Today is a busy day, we have a ceremony to prepare for."

Her words send a sinking feeling to the pit of my stomach, and I feel my complexion pale in response.

"Don't look so frightened, my cousin won't bite," Marisa reassures me, as she turns towards the closet. "That is, until you want him to," she adds teasingly, hinting at the inevitable marking that comes with being mates.

"Right..." I reply awkwardly. For a brief moment, I had managed to forget about the implications of mates.

Opening the closet, Marisa immediately begins rummaging through the clothes. "I can tell you're still in your bathrobe," she remarks, glancing back at me and gesturing towards the silky rope with her head.

"Yeah, I kind of fell asleep wearing it," I confess. The truth is, after my encounter with Legion, I had felt so self-conscious that I had quickly given up on my closet rummage, as it was overwhelming and confusing and had instead hidden under the covers and eventually drifted off to sleep.

"Haven't even had breakfast yet I assume?" She questions and I shake my head in response.

"No dinner either?" She continues to question as she spots the still full tray of food from yesterday. That's when I realize I've been so caught up on all the new impressions that I hadn't even noticed how hungry I was. I shake my head again and she lifts a confused brow.

We only ate the bare necessities on our journey so it's been a while since I've even had proper food. My stomach growls on cue, begging me for some attention.

"Margaret!" Marisa yells out of nowhere and I jump a bit. The door opens within a few seconds to reveal the same woman who prepared my bath yesterday.

"Yes?" She asks eagerly.

"Can you be a dear and fetch some food for our lovely Willow." Marisa sounds polite as she addresses Margaret.

Margaret nods her head in a respectful manner and leaves the room.

I stare wide eyed at the exchange before I exit the bed, Im not used to servants. Marisa goes back to her search for clothes. I take a seat on the couch that Marisa had sat on yesterday and watch with attentive eyes, hoping that she'll find something I can wear in a hurry because I failed in that gigantic maze of a closet.

Despite only being in a robe, I don't feel as vulnerable in her presence as I did around Legion. Maybe thats just because my hair was wet and I was cold though...

"This would look great on you!" Marisa exclaims, her voice filled with excitement as she presents me with a light blue dress adorned with golden accents that shimmer in the light. It exudes a royal aura, as if it's a garment meant for someone other than myself.

"I don't know if it would fit me," I hesitantly respond.

She throws me a deadpan expression. "If you're referring to the size, which you better be, you're mistaken. It will fit you perfectly."

●~●~●~●~●~●~●~●~●~●

I stand before a golden mirror, my reflection revealing a woman who feels both thrilled and out of place. The light blue dress with delicate golden accents, hugs my body in a way that accentuates my features. It's elegant and beautiful, yet I can't help but feel like an imposter wearing it.

As I look at myself an uneasy feeling washes over me. The dress is breathtaking, no doubt, but it feels too royal for someone like me. I'm accustomed to simpler attire, clothes that blend seamlessly with the surroundings of my village not with this castle. So in a way I'm thankful to able to bend in with the castles people in this dress, but perhaps I should try a less elegant dress first.

I turn to Marisa, my voice filled with uncertainty. "I... I don't know if I should be wearing this." I drop head slightly feeling ashamed.

Marisa's eyes soften with understanding, her tone gentle. "Willow, the dress suits you, even if it feels different. Embrace this moment, embrace the change it represents." She places a warm hand on my arm.

I try to dim the unpleasant feeling and instead find strength to step outside of my comfort zone, yet I still feel my breakfast, which Margaret had fetched in record time, turn in my stomach as I look at myself.

Marisa senses my hesitation and offers a comforting smile. "Take a moment to breathe, Willow. We've still got much to do. When you're ready, we can proceed with picking a ceremony dress."

Nodding silently, I try to gather my thoughts and not let my fears take over but the room still feels suffocating.

"I... think I need some air," I finally admit, my voice barely above a whisper. "I'd like to walk alone and explore the castle. It might help me... settle more in."

Marisa nods with soft eyes. "Of course, Willow. Take all the time you need. But not too much." She says with a wink.

With a grateful smile, I make my way out of the room, my steps cautious and uncertain. I close the door behind me and lean against it for a brief moment as I close my eyes and exhale deeply.

The moment is over in a flash as I quickly become aware of the fact that the halls aren't empty. I try to gain my composure as I straighten out and walk along but curious eyes follow my every step, making me feel increasingly on edge.

I continue to walk, hoping to find a place void of people but every turn I take down the halls reveals another set of eyes. The weight of their stares presses down on me, and my steps quicken in response to the mounting anxiety. Each turn I take seems to reveal more prying eyes, intensifying the stress I feel. I also hear the increasing chatter behind me and I instinctively lower my gaze in hopes that less people will notice my foreign face.

In an attempt to find some refuge from the suffocating scrutiny, I stumble into a room that seems vacant due to the dark atmosphere around it.

It takes me a moment to confirm that it is in fact vacant, after my eyes adjust to the darkness. I scan the rest of the room with my newly adjusted eyesight. In the center stands a towering statue of a man, casting its menacing shadow across the marble floor. Its presence commands attention, and for a moment a chill runs down my spine and I shiver as I inhale.

And if that wasn't enough a deep voice from behind startles me. "That's King Octavius," the voice announces, I jump and turn around, only to find Finley emerging from the hallway, the place where I had just entered as well.

"He was a great ruler, deeply respected." He continues as he finds his place next to me. "But also ruthless and feared."

I swallow the lump in my throat, feeling a nervousness creep up inside me. This is the man who murdered the previous white wolf. He lived within these walls, and now I do too...

The statue reminds me that a simple mistake could cause me my life. If my wolf emerges just once my life is doomed. My own mate could be my downfall... at least if he's anything like his father.

"You look a little pale, Willow. Are you alright?" Finley squints his eyes, and I avert my gaze, feeling uneasy.

"I'm fine. It's all just very overwhelming," I struggle to catch my breath as I respond.

Finley remains silent for a moment before speaking again. "I noticed. You should really keep your head up as you walk the halls."

I glance back at Finley, and he continues. "Don't let them see you weak."

I nod and look back at the enamours statue. It's hard to understand that this man was really the father of Legion, yet also makes so much sense. I begin to wonder if Legion will also have a statue that big or if he perhaps already has one, unless you only get one for killing white wolves.

I rip my eyes away from the man in stone and return my eyes to Finley with a new question dancing on my lips.

"How did the king pass?" I inquire, unable to ignore the sense of mystery surrounding his sudden death. At my question Finley tenses up visibly.

"Heart attack." he responds curtly.

Intuitively, I sense that there is more to the story, a deeper truth concealed behind his words. However, for now, I decide to let it go, knowing that further probing may yield little. Instead, I shift the conversation toward a different sensitive subject.

"You mentioned that the king was brutal during our journey. Did his brutality extend to Legion as well?" I ask cautiously.

Finley snorts at my question. "So many questions, once again," He says hinting at my earlier interrogation surrounding the creature we had encountered.

Recognizing the need for patience, I remain silent as I wait for his response to my question.

"Legion's father believed in strict discipline, which often included punishments for his son," Finley's voice carries an undertone of sadness.

An ache stirs within my heart at his words. Determined to understand more, I press on, seeking greater clarity. "Punishments? What kind of punishments did he endure?" I want to know about Legion's past for a fairly innocent reason, besides my natural curiosity, it could mean coming closer to understanding him more.

Finley's face tightens, his lips forming a thin line. It becomes evident that he isn't willing to disclose any further details about the punishments. I want to ask more, to know every detail but at the same time, the silence is almost an answer in itself and suddenly I'm not even sure if I really do want the details, so I drop it.

Finley's reticence towards my questions must stem from a place of respect and loyalty towards Legion. I begin to wonder if these two men are closer than you'd assume at first glance. I know you must respect your king but it seems like much more than the loyalty to a king. A respect for a friend perhaps?

With a heavy sigh, I nod as a response. Maybe, in time, Legion will be the one to answer my questions, however with how stubborn and distrusting he is, I find that hard to believe. I suppose I must settle for those around him for now.

Finley excuses himself with a nod and turns to depart the room leaving me alone with my thoughts and the looming statue of King Octavius.

As I stand in the room, surrounded by the stillness, I can't help but wonder again if Legion is anything like his father, and if he is then what does that mean for me? Doom?

Feeling eerie in the stoney presence of King Octavius I also leave the room. I'd gladly take the prying eyes over the murderous ones belonging to the statue.

•~•~•~•~•~•~•~•~•~•

I hurry and try to make my way back to my room but the halls are just as confusing as they were yesterday. People still murmur upon seeing me venture the halls but I remind myself of Finleys advice and keep my head up. I feel somewhat more confident now, it's as if running into the great King Octavius was enough to put things into perspective, none of these people are truly a threat to me... yet.

Lost in thought about my many worries I fail to evade a heavy collision with my shoulder, as someone walks into me, though it felt a bit too harsh too seem like an accident. I turn quickly to see who crashed into me, not that it made me stumble, or even hurt, seeing as I have supernatural strength but it definitely got my attention.

I'm met with a face full of disdain and eyes with fury belonging to a woman with brown curly hair. Confused I come to a halt and investigate the woman further.

She's shorter than me but tall enough to make the clash with my shoulder. The rage in her eyes adds an intimidating edge. "Do they not teach you manners where you come from?" Her words pierce the air, drawing audible gasps from the onlookers who have now stopped in their tracks, their attention fixated on our confrontation. No longer pretending to be doing something other than stalking me with their eyes.

Baffled I open my mouth to speak but my mind doesn't follow along as it still scrabbles to find the words to respond.

"Are you mute?" She continues probing and my eyes widen due to her sheer rudeness.

Caught off guard and not knowing what to say I try to force some semblance of a response out. "No... I... I..."

In an instant, the woman's expression changes dramatically, draining all color from her face. The surrounding crowd falls into a sudden and eerie silence. The woman is no longer looking at me, and I follow her line of view curious to see what has evoked such frightened reaction. As I turn around to where her eyes are glued, I'm surprised to find Legion behind me with his arms crossed and a hard stare.

His strikingly silver eyes are glaring directly at the woman and although he is usually impossible to read, It's clear that there's an anger within them this time. I'm grateful that I'm not of the receiving end of this stare. I'm sure it's enough to make your skin crawl uncontrollably. The sight of him makes my heartbeat rise slightly and I wonder if hers is beating at all.

"Excuse me Your Highness." The woman stammers almost inaudible and I look back at her just in time to witness her scurry along in a panicked matter.

As my gaze finds its way back to Legion his eyes also shift to lock with mine. I notice a slight softening in his features, a subtle shift that brings me slight comfort, happy that it isn't me he's upset with.

A pleasant feeling starts welling up within me. It feels like relief and I understand that I'm not just relived but grateful that he has helped me end this uncomfortable exchange.

"Willow." Legion says breaking the tension. His eyes shift again this time traveling down my body taking in the dress I'm wearing while scanning the details of it.

I begin to wonder if he still remembers the robe from yesterday but quickly try to think of something else as I feel my cheeks heat up.

As if to make matters worse, I become painfully aware of the dress that I'm wearing and how it's too tight on my body for my liking. His eyes linger longer than I had wished. Maybe he finally sees that I look misplaced here, just like I feel. But he doesn't say anything, he simply clenches his jaw and reconnects our eyes.

His eyes have darkened again with something. Something I realize that I've seen before yesterday even, like when we were in the lake, but perhaps it's just leftover anger from the previous encounter.

I feel a semblance of electricity spark in my fingertips and I avert my gaze in an instant. It's as if my body is speaking a language I've yet to understand.

"Legion." I reply as I swiftly move past him to escape what must be the trickery of the bond.

It must be...

__________________________________A/N

Almost time for a ceremony now...

What did y'all think of the mean woman? Any guesses as to what her problem was?

If you still enjoy the story I'd appreciate it if you clicked on the star (and also on my other chapters if you haven't already □) it just helps a ton!

See ya guys later! I got a lot more chapters!

CHAPTER 11 - REMEDY

I return to my room with a pounding heart and as I open the door all sorts of fabrics overflow the room. The room is stuffed with extravagant dresses and an even more ecstatic Marisa than when I left, if that's even possible.

Marisa isn't the only person in the room anymore either, there's more people and their chattering come to a halt upon seeing me.

"There you are." Marisa exclaims walking over to greet me by grabbing both my hands in a tight squeeze. "I was scared you had gotten lost or worse, ran away." She chuckles and returns her eyes to the many people.

"Now, I've gathered you all here to prepare a ceremony so let's start with the ceremonial dresses shall we."

They all bow their head a bit with a smile to acknowledge her request. These people seem to like Marisa based on their relaxed faces and even happy expressions.

One of the women step forward and directs her attention to me as she speaks. "Your Highness, we've made a variety of ceremonial dresses for you-"

"You... made these?" I accidentally interrupt the woman as I'm taken aback with astonishment. I'm quick to realize how rude it is to interrupt so I lower my head and apologize. "I'm sorry, it's just that I arrived yesterday..."

The women all look at each other with knowing smiles before someone responds. "We started making them the second we heard the news of The Kings mate."

It dawns on my that the women made these grand dresses in much less than 24 hours. "That must've been very difficult, I'm sorry." I reply feeling a bit embarrassed that they went through all that trouble just because of me.

I glance at the dresses again, they all look like they should've taken at least a week to prepare because of the intricate and detailed design. They're all unique in their own way but they all share two things in common: they're white and have a lot of fabric trailing behind them.

"Stop apologizing Your Highness, we were extremely happy when we heard the news. It's a miracle that we're honored to be a part of." The woman continues and I furrow my brows at the word miracle.

Marisa chimes in before I can question the word. "But alas you can only wear one, so which one will it be?"

•~•~•~•~•~•~•~•~•~•

Marisa and I am alone and once again. I'm peering into the golden mirror but this time the dress doesn't fit within the frame fully, not even to mention how heavy it is. However it is undeniably gorgeous. The beautiful white gown delicately embraces my figure, accentuating the curves of my body and complimenting my slim waistline. It exudes an irresistible allure.

The gown has a bare neckline that frames my shoulders, leaving them bare while showing off my collarbone. The dress also has some exquisite lacework sleeves that add even more elegance to the already incredible dress.

But the most captivating element of the gown is its magnificent train, flowing behind me. The train seems to stretch on endlessly, like a waterfall of fabric.

The layers of soft fabric and delicate silk create a dreamlike illusion, as if I'm floating on air.

As I stand in this mesmerizing white dress, a mixture of nerves and excitement courses through my veins. The approaching ceremony looms in the back of my mind, filling me with both anticipation and anxiety. The gown's beauty however does serve as a reminder of the seriousness about all of this. This is truly happening, and on top of it, in front of a lot of people.

Yet, even amidst my apprehension, I can't help but admire at the details of the dress, like the bare shoulders and the lacework that adorns the sleeves. It is truly a magnificent garment, which yet again makes me feel like I should not be wearing it.

I let out a sigh and turn towards Marisa, but she swiftly interrupts any protests I may have. "Don't start, Willow. It's a beautiful dress on a beautiful woman."

Nervously, I fiddle with my hands and respond, "It feels a bit much, and I'm not sure I can even walk properly in this."

Marisa rolls her eyes. "Practicality isn't the aim here. This dress is meant to take your breath away, to create a sense of magic and wonder, just like you, the new Queen and Luna."

Her words make me visibly cringe and I leave the frames of the mirror in an attempt to make my way to the couch, but I fail miserably in my efforts. The weight of the dress feels as though heavy weights are attached to its fabric.

"We're going to have to do something about that walk." Marisa mumbles to herself.

She observes me with a hint of amusement dancing in her eyes as I continue the challenging task of reaching the couch. After what feels like an eternity of awkward struggle, I manage to position myself in a way that allows me to practically throw myself onto the soft red cushions.

The dress isn't the only thing weighing me down however. The awaiting ceremony has created a pit of worry in my stomach that doesn't dissolve no matter what I do or think of.

Marisa follows suit and takes a seat beside me on the couch. I continue to fidget with my hands, my mind overrun with relentless worries that roam freely, entangling my thoughts in their grip

"Why did it have to be so soon?" I question hinting at the ceremony.

Marisa puts one of her hands over mine to stop my fidgeting as she replies, "it has to be on a full moon, which is tomorrow, I doubt my cousin could wait another month for this miracle to be sealed completely."

And there it is again, the word miracle. I frown as I turn to face Marisa. "What is up with that word? Why do you all say that?"

Marisas face is painted with a hint of confusion as she replies, "what? Miracle?"

"Yes!" I eagerly say. "That word! Why miracle? It is quite normal to have a mate." I state matter-of-factly.

Marisa stays silent for a bit as if even more confused by my reaction so I proceed with a tone matching her bewilderment. "Or... do you guys not have those here often?"

Marisa finally breaks her confused exterior and lets a smile grace her lips. "Of course we have mates Willow. I would personally consider my dear Ellie a miracle, but that is not why we're saying that."

I slouch further down in despair and drop my gaze as I realize my place here is still totally unclear to me. I have no idea what I'm doing or supposed to do, I'm not even sure how to act or what's considered rude. My run-in, quite literally, with that woman only confused me further. Is that how people act here? If so I'm not sure I'll ever get used to it.

"Willow," she starts, breaking my worrisome thoughts. "When Legion turned 18 and he still hadn't found his mate people grew worried, then a year passed and nothing, then another and another and it continued like that until people gave up hope and believed that only a miracle could grant him a mate."

I return my eyes to Marisa slowly and she takes it as a cue to proceed. "Legions father said he was being punished by the Moon Goddess for whatever reason and when the king... passed, it stuck around. A cursed King doomed to live alone. No one knew why, but no one dared question it." Her eyes become glossy as she talks and as if even possible my hate for the previous King doubles. For the first time my hate for King Octavius seems greater than my fear for him.

She shuts her eyes and takes a deep breath, then continues. "Legion, much like his father, didn't believe he'd ever get a mate and he definitely didn't believe in some miracle that one day he'd be granted one." Marisa opens her eyes again. I feel her pain as she stares into mine. I feel that pain expand to Legion.

"You must understand that you are a miracle to us, and especially Legion, because he never even thought you existed Willow." She speaks with a soft and comforting voice.

Awkwardly, I shift in my seat after hearing Marisa's words. I feel ignorant, almost as if all my reasons for disliking Legion have been swept away with a single story. A story that resonates with me as well, making it all the more impactful...

I also lost hope of getting a mate somewhere along the way. Now I feel stupid for questioning the word miracle. To me it also felt impossible that I'd have a mate, so when I met Legion I was in denial and too caught up on my fear of being discovered to see what our bond meant outside of my possible death.

My eyes flicker around as it dawns on me that Legion has, just like me, thought he was doomed to a lifetime of loneliness.

His persistence and actions when we first met now make sense. As much as I want to keep blaming him, it's like I can't anymore. He simply couldn't let his chance at happiness get away.

Even from the beginning I understood not wanting to leave a mate behind or lose them, but now it feels as if my eyes have been opened up to a completely new world. One where Legion and I are alike. A world where loneliness is our greatest weakness and where the hope of ever suffocating the feeling once felt impossible.

I feel a tug at my heart as I come to the realization that I've known it all along. I knew we were alike when I decided to go with him, even if I put up some resistance, I did go with him in the end, because on the inside I knew, or maybe hoped that he could be the remedy to my loneliness. The only one I'd ever get...

"Are you okay Willow?" Marisa questions with concern lingering in her tone.

"Yeah I just need some air, can you help me get out of this?" I reply trying to fake a smile to convey that I'm feeling better than I am.

Marisa doesn't question me further and instead helps me as I requested. Once I can get out of the dress myself, she turns around to give me privacy and I swiftly step out of it and put on the dress from before.

Marisa shows me to a balcony that's connected to my room and excuses herself to allow me to have some alone time.

Time passes but I still feel dizzy standing on the balcony. I eagerly try to inhale as much air as possible, but no matter how much I seem to inhale it just won't fill my lungs completely.

My new revelation has completely taken my breath away, yet I also feel a sense of relief as it feels like I'm one step closer to understanding Legion. I know there's still a long way and it's going to be difficult getting into his head, but I have to try, he is my mate after all.

With a new determination I decide to seek out Legion. I have to see him before the ceremony tomorrow. I owe it to the moon goddess to respect her mates, and perhaps a part of me is also drawn to him.

I walk into the room again where Marisa has been waiting for me and she turns around upon hearing me return.

"I need you to take me to Legion."

•~•~•~•~•~•~•~•~•

I must admit that it seemed like a better idea to speak with Legion in my room than now that I'm standing outside of his door. I can't help but tremble slightly. The weight of my newfound knowledge weighs down on me, and I feel a tremor of uncertainty.

"I know you're there Willow." Legion's commanding voice cuts through the silence, booming through the door. My breath catches in my throat. Now I also wish Marisa would've stayed but she left shortly after showing me to his quarters, saying that this was between him and me. And she is right of course.

Summoning all the courage I can muster, I push open the heavy doors, revealing Legion seated behind a big wooden desk. His eyes meet mine with question, waiting for me to state my purpose here.

As my silence proceeds, his gaze intensifies, an unspoken demand for me to speak. A slight furrow forms between his brows, a subtle sign of his growing curiosity. "Close the door behind you, Willow," he orders.

Shakily, I comply turning slowly to shut the heavy doors behind me. The sound of the latch clicking into place resonates through the room, creating a sense of seclusion and intimacy. The reality of the moment settles upon me, and I find myself at an even greater loss for words, my mind racing to find the right thing to say. Before I can even face him again, the faint sound of Legion rising from his seat reaches my ears.

As I pivot back, my eyes meet Legion's firm figure, leaning casually against the front of his desk, his arms confidently crossed. His eyes sweep over the dress I'm wearing yet again, studying it for a moment before meeting my eyes with a slight mix of apology and understanding. "I apologize for Cathrine." he declares, his words tinged with an unexpected humility and slight softness.

Confusion laces my voice as I question, "What?" Then, realization dawns, and I swiftly recall the encounter with the rude woman. "Oh, her," I interject before he has a chance to respond.

Legion nods. "Indeed, I assure you it won't happen again." His eyes are sharp with a seriousness entangled in them.

"Thank you, but that's not why I'm here." I finally say. Determination fills my voice as I steer the conversation back on track, focusing on what truly matters.

Legion, ever composed, tilts his head slightly, a signal for me to elaborate further. With that I finally delve into my true intentions for coming here. "The ceremony is merely a day away, and I had a few questions."

His exterior softens up and the confusion leaves his face but he still remains silent allowing me to continue with no interruptions.

Summoning my courage, I lower my gaze momentarily, gathering my thoughts before meeting Legion's eyes once more. Nervousness courses through me, well aware that I'm about to touch on a sensitive subject. Nonetheless, I press on, wanting to express my intentions clearly.

"I think," I begin cautiously, "I think we should get to know each other before the ceremony."

As my words hang in the air, Legion reacts by uncrossing his arms and instead placing them firmly on the desk, his hands gripping the edge. The surprise in his voice is evident as he responds, "You want to get to know me?" His disbelief at my willingness to bond with him is obvious. It's probably unexpected given our history of constant resistance.

However, I stand my ground, unwavering in my determination, and maintain eye contact, refusing to look away. "Yes," I affirm resolutely.

I see a hint of a smile grace his lips but before I can be sure, it's gone, leaving me unsure if I imagined it or not. "Alright, then let me ask you this, how come you were in that forest the day we met?"

His question catches me off guard, and confusion clouds my mind for a moment. I blink rapidly, trying to collect myself as my nerves flare up. "Because I like being alone." I shoot back hurriedly.

He still hasn't forgotten about that...

An anxious shiver runs down my spine.

He narrows his eyes at my hastily response, ready to dig deeper into my answer, but I can't let that happen.

"My turn," I interject, my words tumbling out faster than he can question me. "What were you doing there, so far from your kingdom?"

It wasn't my intent to start an interrogation, I genuinely wanted to get to know him but of course Legion can't just be nice for once.

"Royal business." He curtly responds. The growing tension between us is evident as his hands grip tighter onto the edge of the desk.

"Which I am now." I retort smugly.

He snorts dismissively, "Technically not until tomorrow." His words catch me off guard, and my mouth falls open slightly, taken aback by his remark. But he presses on, his demeanor shifting, becoming more intense.

"Why are you suppressing your wolf?" Legion's question hits me like a punch to the gut, and horror washes over me.

"What?" I manage to utter, my heart pounding.

Legion straightens up and walks closer, slowly closing the distance between us. My instincts kick in, and I instinctively take a step back, creating space between us.

"I can feel your wolf," he states firmly, his gaze fixed on me. "Why are you shutting it out?" His proximity sends shivers down my spine and I take a few more small steps backwards.

"I... I'm not," I stutter, trying to deny the accusation. But a slight smirk forms on his lips, making me feel a growing frustration course through me. The intensity in the air hangs heavy, like a storm about to break.

"What was that creature?" I urgently press desperate to divert the focus from his probing questions. His once smug expression dissipates in an instant, replaced by a stern and serious countenance, indicating I may have struck a nerve. I feel the sense of a small victory at his shift.

His jaw clenches tightly but instead of backing down, he strides forward until he's right in front of me. My heart races, the proximity accentuating his powerful presence. "Danger." He simply states in a low voice. His words sound like a warning and I shiver inwardly.

Despite my urge to retreat, I stand my ground, resolute not to let him intimidate me. "Why were you certain you were doomed to a life without a mate?" I venture into a different line of questioning, hoping he might offer some answers at least.

As if even possible he moves closer to me in response, his presence now almost intoxicating. I peer up at him, still staying in my spot and he looks down at me with a tensed demeanor. "Perhaps for the same reason you were." He finally responds, his voice a husky rumble that sends a thrill through me. I struggle to maintain my composure in our close proximity

I'm uncertain of what he means by that but something in me prevents me from probing further, as if I know it'll have consequences. He continues to stare into my eyes with his piercing silver orbs and we both stay silent while starring each other down.

After some time he places his hand on my lower back and I stand still awaiting his next move. Then he speaks with an alluring voice. "I could mark you right now." I tense up upon hearing his words but I remain still nonetheless as my heart seems to skip a beat.

He uses his other hand to brush my hair away from my shoulder, revealing my neck. "Do you want that Willow?" Electricity runs through my body at his action leaving me breathless with anticipation.

Legion leans in closer and for a moment, I find myself speechless, wondering if Catherine was right, perhaps I am mute. I even instinctively close my eyes and tilt my head, allowing him easier passage.

I internally curse myself yet nothing changes and my eyes remain closed as I am anticipating his next move.

He seems to like my body's response to his actions as his hand on my back pulls me in closer with a firm grip.

_______________________________A/N

Cliffhanger?? Hehe sorry guys, took some time to edit this as summer got busy but I promise I'm working on all the chapters as you read this!

As always if you like the story click the star! Doesn't hurt ya;) and it helps me a lot. Don't be scared to comment I love to talk:)

A/N: Just a Little Update

Hi guys I promise I'm working on the next chapter however I've been very busy as I'm currently in a completely different continent and I've been traveling around. My summer has been great and quite busy but I have not forgotten y'all and I'm working on chapters whenever I can.

The next chapter will be posted sometime this week and I hope y'all are stoked for it! So until then I'd love to talk to you guys in the comments or just answer a question.

I'd also LOVE to hear what's your fave moment between Legion and Willow so far?

What's your fave moment overall?

Who's your fave character?

And at last which chapter/chapters you liked the most?

CHAPTER 12 - KNOCKS

Suddenly a knock interrupts Legion and me as it sounds through the big doors. Legion pulls back as I open my eyes in shock scared that someone may find us in this vulnerable position. I push Legion away even further but he doesn't budge at all and instead the force sends me back stumbling.

Legion sighs clearly frustrated as he wearily press the bridge of his nose. "Not now!" He commands loudly and the intruder outside hastily retreats, obedient to his order.

He turns is focus back to me his demeanor now tensed and without wasting a moment, I speak quickly before he can say another word that might put me in a trance like the one I had just been in.

"I have to go." I try to assert but almost stumble over my words as I hurriedly talk. Legion opens his mouth to reply but I cut him off. "And I really did mean it when I said I wanted to get to know you."

A subtle transformation sweeps over Legion as my words reach him, softening his eyes along with his rigid exterior and I turn to leave. My steps feel heavy as I make my way towards the doors saddened that my plan failed so miserably.

As I approach the doors, ready to exit, Legions voice cuts through the air. "My mother died giving birth to me." His tone is gentle, very unlike Legions usual cold and harsh one.

I come to a halt shocked by his words. As I stand there silent and taken aback, I grapple with how to respond to his revelation. Just as I'm processing his disclosure, he speaks once more. "Your turn."

I take a deep breath steadying myself before I turn around to face Legion. His eyes find mine within a second and I'm immediately overwhelmed by the intensity of his gaze. Feeling a rush of vulnerability, I instinctively try to evade direct eye contact, it's as if his stare has the power to see right through me.

I internally struggle for a few moments. "My father disappeared before I was born." I finally find the courage to speak. "Or rather left us." I quickly correct myself with a solemn tone.

Despite never having met my father it's still something that cuts deep. He didn't even have a chance to meet me before he decided I was unwanted... It's a void that haunts me, a missing piece of my identity that leaves me with unanswered questions.

Legion breaks our eye contact for the first time, looking to the side with tight brows as if in deep thought before meeting my gaze again. Perhaps these types of conversations are too much for him?

I scan his face for more emotion that might reveal what is causing such sudden reaction but find none.

"We don't have to do this." I offer in an attempt to make him more comfortable as he seems out of his element.

I've never seen Legion break eye contact before...

He doesn't say anything for what feels likes an eternity with a somewhat puzzled look on his face, however it's always hard to tell with that man. Just as I begin to wonder if he'll speak again, he finally opens his mouth."As you already know, thanks to Finley, my dad was an..." he hesitates, searching for the right words, "interesting man."

As soon as Finley's name escapes his lips, guilt surges through me like a relentless tide. I can't shake the fact that I've gone behind Legion's back, not once, but twice. Avoiding direct eye contact, I avert my gaze, fearing he'd catch a glimpse of my remorseful expression, betraying the sorry guilt gnawing at my conscience

When I don't say anything he continues. "He-"

Another knock interrupts him and he immediately goes silent and shuts his eyes in frustration, trying to contain his annoyance before responding to the disturbance with a sharp, "Yes!?" His voice carry an irritated tone as he directs his attention to the doors.

The doors open like clockwork and I jolt aside to give Legion full view of whoever it might be. The doors reveal one of his men with blonde hair who's name I don't know. He looks at me briefly and his brows furrow in confusion but he quickly shakes it off and directs his attention to Legion. He doesn't say anything however, he just looks at him like he's communicating his purpose with a single glance and Legion simply nods once and turns to me.

I peak my head up awaiting his words. "I'll have someone escort you back to your room Willow." His tone is nothing but professional and I know it's a sign that our tender moment is lost.

I don't protest as it seems pointless. Whatever has gotten Legions attention is clearly important and not something I wish to interfere with. As if conjured by magic a woman appears a few moments after, practically having nerves and anxiety painted all over her face. I suppose I'd also look like that if I worked for Legion. Working for Legion must come with its own set of pressures. I can't help but empathize, knowing that I probably wear a similar expression half the time, especially now, as I am about to become his queen. The weight of my impending role adds to the sense of unease lingering in the air.

She gestures for me to come with her and I do so. Yet I can't help but to turn my head one last time before the doors close behind us. Legions gaze is already piercing through me with an intense look in his eyes that I've never seen before. It feels more urgent than ever but before I can analyze it further the doors slam shut, sending echos through the halls.

●~•~•~•~•~•~•~•~•~•~•

Marisa is no longer in my room when I return, instead I find a note saying that she is off planing my grand ceremony and a few warnings about the odd nature of the ceremony.

I put the note down and sigh. Just when it felt like I got somewhere with Legion we were interrupted. If it isn't us sabotaging ourselves, it's someone else.

Plus tomorrow marks the day that I become the Luna and Queen yet it still feels like my mate is a complete stranger, sure there was a small moment today where he opened up, but it wasn't nearly enough to claim that I truly know him.

Deciding that I need a distraction, I begin searching the vast room for something to occupy my mind. The shelves hold an array of books, but none of them manage to pique my interest. The balcony only offers so much of a distraction, the view is mesmerizing but it's almost as if the view is too much to handle, as if everything is more real when I stand there peering over the kingdom.

I run my fingertips over the walls along with the different furniture as I take laps around the room hoping to find something that'll make time pass by quicker. However I find nothing and after my second lap I give up defeated.

As if on cue, a gentle knock resonates at my door. For a fleeting moment, I catch myself hoping it might be Legion, but I quickly quash that wishful thought. I shake my head, dismissing any unrealistic fantasies, and soon recognize the more plausible truth, it's likely Marisa returning to delve into further planning.

"Come in," I say, expecting Marisa, but to my surprise, it's not her at the door. Instead, it's the woman who prepared my bath yesterday, Margaret, if I recall correctly.

"I'm sorry Your Highness, I just wanted to prepare your bath for the evening." Her tone is soft.

"It's already so late?" I sound startled as I turn to look out the window only to be met with a sun ready to set. Today has been quite the eventful day making it pass faster than I had expected. This means I'm even closer to the inevitable ceremony. I feel my nerves spike at the mere thought.

"Indeed Your Highness." Margaret responds looking puzzled by my reaction.

When I don't respond immediately, she hesitantly continues, "Would you like me to prepare the bath... before the dinner is served in the dining hall?" Her voice is gentle and cautious, as if afraid of intruding.

At that she gains my attention. "Dinning hall?" My tone matches my confusion.

She looks at me like I just spoke in a foreign language but answers me nonetheless. "You know a room where you eat Your Highness."

"Call me Willow." I wave my hand in a dismissive manner. "And I'm well aware but who will I be eating with?" I wasn't even aware that this place had anything that even resembled a place to socialize.

"I apologize Your Highness." She looks down at her shoes in embarrassment and I sigh inwardly at the title I'm unable to shake. "I'm not sure if The King will be joining but many of the the other royals will along with the families of the court and pack." She still sounds even more timid now.

"I would like a bath." I simply state.

•~•~•~•~•~•~•~•~•~•

The bath was swift, as an unusual motivation to interact with the people of the castle took hold of me for the first time. I'm not entirely sure what sparked this newfound desire. It could be the eagerness to prepare myself for the upcoming ceremony by meeting some of the people attending or perhaps because I want to get to know the people that I will soon be the Queen and Luna of. Or maybe even a third option: I want to meet the people closest to Legion. But I avoid regarding the last option as valid. I'm sure I'm just in a social mood for the first time ever.

Marisa paid me a visit in my room to assist in choosing an outfit and accompany me to the dining hall. She had asked Margaret to keep her informed about my attendance and was delighted to hear that I would be joining. Apparently these dinners are a frequent thing I can look forward to.

Her choice was a tight-fitting burgundy dress that I worried would draw too much attention. However, much like before, Marisa convinced me that it was fitting for a Queen. Thankfully, the dress still retained its flowing silhouette with a looser skirt, which provided some comfort as it concealed parts of my figure. Yet, the fabric seemed to betray me as it hugged my body tightly regardless.

"Where do I even sit?" I question lowly as Marisa and I make our way towards the dining hall. We're running a bit late which was only made clear to me after countless minutes of arguing over her choice of dress for me.

"At the end of the table." She replies confidently and I stare back at her in horror. "Maybe?" She adds with an amused smile, as if it's helpful in any way at all.

I stop dead in my tracks and Marisa immediately grabs my arm and hurries me along. "Don't worry Willow you'll do great." She sound enthusiastic.

"I don't know..." I hesitate but before I can't get another word out she turns us to face two large doors with loud sounds of people emerging from behind them.

"Here we are." She wastes no time as she knocks on the door twice preventing me from protesting more.

I shut my mouth in anticipation as the large doors open. A bright light immediately greets us as the shine from the dinning hall breaks through first along with chatter and I soon after notice a long table with what feels like hundreds of people seated.

As Marisa leads me inside through the doors the room falls into a hush. Every head turns in our direction, and the weight of their collective gaze feels suffocating. Regret washes over me for listening to Marisa's choice of dress, as it seems like they're all scrutinizing it.

Despite the discomfort, I force myself to push through the feeling and take in the scene before me. The room is filled with countless unfamiliar faces, and Legion is nowhere to be seen. Both grand chairs at the ends of the long table remain vacant. The table itself is adorned with an abundance of food, enough to feed my entire village, and my mouth waters at the sight of it.

Marisa leans towards my ear. "You sit at the left end." Her voice is low and subtle and I nod ever so slightly before I turn to walk to my seat, parting ways with Marisa who apparently sits nowhere near me. I really don't wish to sit at the center of attention but causing a scene would undoubtedly be much worse, so I simply bite my lip as a man pulls out my seat once I'm close enough. He waits for me to sit down and when I do so he pushes the big chair into place again, now with me in it.

Some of the chattering resumes, however less than before as there's still many curious glances planted on me. Soon after a woman brings me a plate stocked with food.

Feeling like an outsider I look around trying to spot a familiar face and my eyes swiftly finds Marisa, she's sat next to a woman with short brown hair and warm dark skin tone, who I assume to be Ellie. They seem to be deep in conversation as they giggle at something the other said. Both their eyes twinkle with lights as they look at each other and I find myself feeling envious that I'll probably never share such a look with Legion. He'll have to take a break from being a statue with limited poses, and apparently that's not an easy task for the man.

Smiling ever so subtly at my own joke, I shift my gaze elsewhere. Then my eyes find Finley on the opposite side of the table, with a woman next to him who looks just as serious and professional as he usually does. Her hair is black and her eyes green. Finley and the woman aren't talking each other, they're simply eating their food silently, however I do spot Finley placing a comforting hand on hers in between a bite. Even that seems an eternity away from how Legion and I act. He does place the occasional hand on my lower back but it's always to urge me forward into something. Though I'd lie if a said I didn't like it at times, even most of the time...

I shake the thought out of my head and proceed overlooking the table. As my gaze sweeps further over the crowd, I'm met with the angry eyes of Cathrine starring straight at me on the complete opposing end, closely by Legions chair, as if she can send daggers flying at me with her mind. If looks could kill I'd be dead by now with daggers piercing my skin all over.

I cough awkwardly and try to make myself appear smaller as I fill my fork with food to look busy, then I remember Finleys words again and I attempt to fix my posture while putting the fork to my mouth in the most natural way possible.

Cathrines daggers quickly leave my mind as I taste the food. It is so good it almost makes me forget that I'm surrounded by a whole dining hall of prying eyes so I try to keep my attention on the food to make myself more at ease.

After many more bites of the savory food a voice to my right interrupts my chewing. "You must be the beautiful mate of Legion that everyone's been talking so much about." I look up and spot a man directly next to me with a friendly smile plastered on his face. He appears to be early thirties with very dark brown hair on the longer side that almost seems black, but clearly isn't upon further glance.

I nod, ignoring the beautiful part, while trying to swallow the food in my mouth as soon as possible to reply. Finally someone friendly. "Hello I'm Willow." I state trying to look as friendly as possible in return.

His smile broadens. "Well aren't you just the cutest."

My smile fades slightly at the unexpected response.

"This is my mate, Sadie." He redirects my attention to a woman sitting next to him, her hair is platinum blonde. She flashes me a nervous smile.

I nod my head once to greet her and the man speaks again. "Your hair is unlike anything I've seen before. White as snow." This man speaks as if he's airing out his inner thoughts and I feel my smile fading more and more at the nature of this man.

"Oh I apologize where are my manners, my name is Caspian, I'm the first cousin of Legions." He extends his hand and bows his head. I reach out and place my hand in his slowly, painfully aware of our many onlookers. Unexpectedly he rises my hand to his mouth and kisses it gently. The action isn't out of the ordinary but for some reason it startles me. The second he lets go of my hand, I retreat it as if his lips had burned my skin but he remains oblivious to my reaction thankfully. I don't want to make a bad impression...

As I ponder how to respond everyone goes silent again and I look up to see what has triggered such reaction only to find the doors in the middle of opening up. Caspian also turns around to face the doors and we all remain quiet. Soon after Legion emerges through the doors with determined stride. The blonde man from earlier is close behind him.

His steps are powerful and demands the attention he already has. Each step he takes fills up the room with their sound as his feet hit the ground and all eyes remain glued to him. We all watch Legion make his way to his seat with an aura so intense you can't ignore it.

He doesn't address anyone as he sits down, neither does he appear to even look at anyone specific. I shift my gaze to the man behind him, who also happens to be one of the few familiar faces from my journey. He takes a seat close by Legion.

Just as quick as my eyes left Legion they return and I'm surprised to find him gazing straight at me with a look so penetrating it makes Cathrines appear laughable. She should really take intimidation lessons from this man because if it wasn't for our bond I'd think I was in serious trouble.

His gaze shifts and he looks to my side to where his cousin is seated. His eyes shift between us a few times before he peers over the crowd and nods his head. Just like that everyone continues where they left off before he entered the room. They had all been waiting for his permission to proceed which was granted by the nod of his head.

I observe the crowd now that Legion is here. Most people have lowered their voices significantly while others are completely silent. Finley hasn't changed a bit however, still remaining professional. Marisa hasn't changed either I note as her giggles can still be heard through the hall.

Cathrine however isn't burning holes through me anymore. Her intense focus on me seems to have waned, as her gaze now fixates solely on Legion. Her eyes are stuck, as if she fears blinking might cause her to miss even the slightest of his movements.

I roll my eyes and cross my arms, but my self-awareness heightens as I sense two particular pairs of eyes focused intently on me.

I peer around only to find both Caspian and Legion with fixating gazes on me, their unwavering attention making me feel increasingly uneasy.

As my gaze meets Legions he scrunches his eyes as if I've committed some sort of offense, adding to my growing discomfort. Turning to face Caspian bewildered, I notice his once friendly smile has vanished. Instead, he appraises me from head to toe, occasionally glancing back at Legion, creating an atmosphere of tension and uncertainty that leaves me on edge.

I shift in my seat as I try to avoid both of their eyes by keeping my head low and eating my food. I suppose you can't always keep your head up Finley.

_______________________________________A/N

I know I know. Knocks really!? Well don't worry I promise next chapter will be so worth it. What did you think of Legion opening up? What do you think of Caspian? And at last, you liking the tension in the end? As always if you enjoyed the chapter click the star and vote (I reallyyyy appreciate it) and don't be afraid to leave a comment!

CHAPTER 13 - TRUST

The dinner seems to drag on forever as I sit there trying to avoid the glaring gazes from all around me, as if it wasn't enough with Catherine hate filled eyes and the curious ones I had already prepared for prior to the dinner, now I also have to deal with Legions and Caspians.

I'm not sure what has possessed Legion to look at me with such intensity but based on the shift in Caspians eyes when Legion entered, I take it it has something to do with his cousin.

I dare to look up through my lashes though while still keeping my head low. I'm met with the same cold silver eyes looming over me as before so I drop my gaze instantly. A nervous lump forms in my throat as I start to question if I did something to deserve his icy glare.

I also dare to look sideways to see if at least Caspian starring has stopped. Luckily it seems it has, although his eyes are now firmly glued to Legion.

He must've noticed me looking at him however, as his eyes meet mine seconds after and I again drop my gaze swiftly.

Deciding that I've had enough, I hurriedly try to finish my meal. I swallow the food quickly hoping that some of it might take the lump in my throat with it, but alas that doesn't happen. When I'm finally done with my food, I await the perfect time to excuse myself just like I've seen others do throughout the dinner.

The longer I wait the more I start to feel frozen in my place so I simply force my body to stand up after a few moments of building up the courage to do so, hoping that no one will stop me.

Caspian immediately matches my action and gets up as well. He surprisingly takes a hold of my hand as his eyes find mine yet again. "Allow me to walk you out, Your Highness." He sounds respectful despite his odd behavior only moments ago and his harsh eyes have been replaced by casual ones.

I look around nervously before deciding on a reply and realize that many eyes are still on me, including a certain pair that almost seem to be shooting ice. Not wishing to decline him in front of everyone, I ignore Legion and return my attention to him, nodding silently.

A satisfied smirk forms on his face. He then grips my hand tighter as he ushers me along. If it wasn't for Caspians tugging I'm sure I would've been stuck in place.

As we move towards the doors I peer in Legions direction nervous to see his reaction. Just as I anticipated he looks just about ready to break something. I'm not sure what his problem is or if it perhaps is with me...

Legion gets up abruptly not long after I look at him and he heads straight towards us. Caspian doesn't seem to notice as we reach the doors where two guards open them for us, instead his attention is directed towards me. "Shall I follow you to your room as well, Your Highness?" At his question my eyes shift back to Caspian after having been glued to the tensed man heading our way, but before I can decline, Legions voice interrupts us.

"I believe I can take it from here Caspian." His tone matches his exterior and I can sense an anger emanating from him.

Surprised Caspian turns to his cousin who stands tall behind him. Caspian let's go of my hand as a smug expression takes ahold of his face. "Why of course cousin, she's all yours." His voice displays a hint of playfulness in it, one that is clearly meant to provoke.

I don't dare to speak as the two men stand before each other, plus even if I tried I'm sure the lump in my throat would make it difficult.

Looking around it seems I'm not the only one silent. Everyone in the room has become our audience as they watch our exchange unfold before them.

Marisa looks at us with anxious eyes and Finley with angered. Cathrine is however only starring at me with hateful eyes.

I feel my face heat up as embarrassment rushes through me. This is not how I wanted dinner to go, but yet again nothing goes as planned.

Slowly my heartbeat starts thudding harshly throughout my body and that's when I've had enough of this and the glared and the audience. I walk past the two men and hurry out the doors without so much as a word. If they want to cause a scene they can do so without me.

As I hurry down the hall I hear the big doors close behind me. I feel a small moment of relief but that is quickly interrupted by the sound of footsteps following behind me, I can sense that it's Legion. Not wanting to face him after what just happened, I continue my strides and I ignore him.

My plan fails as his hand grabs my wrist less than a minute after, making me come to a halt as his grasp keeps me in place. Legion wastes no seconds before he speaks. "What did you two talk about?" His voice is dripping with disdain.

I narrow my eyes at his question, baffled by his behavior and rip my wrist out of his grip. I look at him for a few more seconds, hoping that he can see just how upset I am by all of it. Then I walk away again wishing that he'll let me be this time.

But he doesn't and instead calls out almost immediately. "Willow." Legions tone is warning and low but I ignore it and pick up my pace.

I feel my embarrassment fade away with each step I take and in it's place an anger grows. Legion doesn't seem to understand that or simply ignores it as he follows close behind.

He doesn't say anything else as he walks behind me but he makes sure to keep up despite my gradual increase in speed.

Minutes after I relax slightly at the sight of my door happy that I could somehow remember the way back. As I reach the door I quickly reach out to grab the handle but his hand grabs mine before I can twist it, preventing me from opening the door. His hand is warm unlike him and I curse myself for liking the way it feels.

Not a word is spoken between us as a tension slowly builds up. He doesn't remove his hand either which confuses my senses as the warmth seems to slowly melt my anger away. I sigh frustrated and turn my head to face him. He's closer than I expected and I flinch internally at the proximity.

He doesn't flinch however, he simply keeps his hand on mine covering it completely with its size and has an impenetrable expression.

"Willow." He says again in a low demanding tone.

"Just like you and me, we barely spoke, now let go." I say with anger. My voice isn't as steady as I'd like though.

His grip around my hand loosens slightly at my words as if what I said had an effect on him. We stay silent for a while, his eyes shifting between mine like he's searching for something. Eventually he clenches his jaw and ultimately lets go.

I waste no seconds as I push open the door, leap into the room and slam it. Had I stayed there longer I'm sure I would have malfunctioned somehow as always.

Feeling grateful that there's now a door between us, I sigh in relief. My hand still holds some of Legions warmth and I flex my hand in response to the lingering feeling.

Now alone in my room it dawns on me that this is my last day before the ceremony and this is how it'll end, I feel some tears press their way forward, stinging my eyes with their presence at the thought. This is how I wanted the day to go.

I suppress them by shutting my eyes harshly, forcing them away. Just as I start to move towards my bed to hide under the covers the door swings back open.

I gasp and whip around in time to see Legion storm through the door frame. He shuts the door behind him and positions himself right in front of me. "We spoke earlier." He states matter of factly.

My first instinct is to push him back out the door but then his words reach my ears. I can't help but retaliate. "We did, and I really felt like I got somewhere with you but then suddenly you didn't have time for me!" I take a determined step forward. This time he won't be the one to corner me

"You're the one who has done nothing but express your displeasure in me." He shoots back within seconds. It's unfair that he can sound so cool and composed compared to me. Then he also steps closer to me, making me feel slightly intimidated but I stand my ground nonetheless.

However his words get to me and I drop part of my defensive facade as I know there's truth to his words. "That was before today." I sound less angry now. "Before I realized..." I trail off as I'm not sure how to end that sentence.

He scrunches his eyebrows for a second as if he didn't expect me to agree with him.

"What?" More of his features soften as everything I said seems to fully dawns on him.

I take a small step backwards and drop my gaze while shaking my head dismissively. He follows and walks closer to me. I keep my head low refusing to meet his eyes, hoping that he'll magically forget what I just said.

Then I feel something touch my chin, gently forcing my face up to look up. "Answer me." He commands and I feel my breath hitch in my throat as I realize that his fingers are holding my chin.

I swallow nervously and my heart picks up it's pace. His fingers are gentle against my skin and I have to stop myself from leaning into his touch. I also try to stop myself from responding but before I know it the words have left my mouth as if beckoned forward by his mere touch.

"Before I realized that you are like me." It's like the world stops for a moment. For a split second he even breaks our eye contact.

Then his eyes soften completely along with his grip while I try to look anywhere but at him. I even try to turn my face but he keeps it in place while starring directly into my eyes with his silver orbs. I start to wonder if he can hear my heartbeat as loudly as I can or if it's just pounding in my ears.

After what feels like an eternity he speaks. "There's certain things I'm trying to shield you from Willow." He looks at me with sincerity. "Just trust me."

"Trust you?" I ask as I pull back and out of his grip. "I barely know you."

He moves even closer despite my clear agitation. "Close your eyes." His voice is gentle now, almost caring. As if that's even possible.

"Did you even hear me." I shoot back, feeling a frustration grow within me again, without his touch to sedate my anger.

"Willow." He says with authority, implicitly demanding me to close my eyes.

And for some reason I do...

With my eyes closed I no the just how silent it is and for a while that all I can hear is Legions soft breathing and my heart beating away, as if it's about to escape my chest, somehow the darkness only fuels my hearts speed.

Soon after I feel Legions hand grab ahold of mine and I jump slightly at the sensation. I instantly want to retreat my hand, as if I had touched a flame. But his grip is secured around me. I feel conflicted as I realize that I don't want him to let go of my hand. The sensation of his hand on mine makes my breathing become heavy like the oxygen in the room has halved.

Then he puts our hands in motion, guiding me and before I can think too much about what he's doing, he places my palm on a hard surface. That's when I feel a thudding beating under my palm. His heart. With my hand placed firmly is on his chest I can feel his heart beating faster than normal and I shutter at the feeling.

Although my eyes are closed, I know they're starting to light up like on the first day we met. I wonder if his are too...

He moves under my palm as he takes a step closer. My eyes still remain closed, it's almost like I'm afraid of opening them now, like I know what might happen if I do. Instead I focus on the feeling of his chest rising and falling along with his breathing. His breathing also seems strained much like my own.

Suddenly I become extra aware of his breathing as I feel it grace my lips. My heart skips a beat at the sensation as I stand there completely still. His other hand finds it's place on my lower back and I press my eyes even more shut overwhelmed by the action. He pulls me a bit closer and our bodies press together.

He breaks the silence. "Feel how your body responds to me... trust or not, you want to be with me." He's basically whispering the words.

Even as we stand there my body is naturally drawn to Legion, obeying his wishes, so I know I can't deny him and I remain silent.

"Just say you want me Willow." His voice is husky. "Say it and you'll get what you want." With each word a breath tickles my lips.

A shiver runs down my spine, along with a now familiar electricity that fills my body, making it tremble. "I..." I try to speak but I'm out of breath and barely audible. Legions hand pulls me closer as if it's even possible and an unbearable heat spreads through my trembling body. His breath on my lips has also sped up, making me infinitely more nervous.

I feel thudding all over my body but I'm not sure if it's my heart of his, causing the sensation.

I take a deep breath trying to steady myself but my body has its own plans and speak on my behalf. "I... do want you." The voice that comes out of my mouth doesn't even sound like me, but I know it's too late. The words have been spoken and there's no taking them back.

His lips collide with mine immediately and my body tenses up at the impact as sparks fly free between. His lips move against mine passionately while his hand drops mine and instead finds my hip. He presses us tightly against each other by pulling me closer. My body still has a mind of its own as my lips naturally start following along with the rhythm of his kiss.

His lips feel soft and plum as the move against mine, they even seem to taste sweet and I question if I'm just imagining things. My body must be rebelling against me because it's making me enjoy the feeling and taste of Legion.

My hands move on their own accord as they start roaming his body by moving up his chest, feeling the solid build underneath my palms. He tenses up slightly in response but then takes it as an invitation to explore my body in return. His hands soon begin to run up and down my sides as if not sure exactly where to go or what to do. His lips remain firmly pressed against mine, moving with a zealous speed and I match it eagerly.

Without breaking our kiss Legions starts moving us backwards and although my body feels stunned with electricity, I follow his move until I'm backed up completely against the bed. Only then does he break our kiss and instead plants his lips on my neck, leaving heated kisses behind. The feeling of his lips on my neck is so intense that I grip his jacket tightly and both push and pull on it.

His kiss deepens upon my reaction and I lean my head back instinctively allowing him more room.

Shortly after his lips leave my neck and my eyes spring open for the first time as both his hands grab a hold of my thighs. With his new hold of me he swiftly lifts me off the ground while starring intensely into my now open eyes.

My heart skips a beat as I meet his gaze mid air and my legs naturally wrap themselves around his hips in response to him lifting me off the ground. My action must come as surprise for Legion because his body becomes rigged against my mine within a second.

Our eyes are both lit up as we stare at each other. I anticipate what he'll do next as I longingly wait for what's to come. Just as it seems he's about to lean in for another kiss, he simply places his forehead on mine and closes his eyes. He's out of breath just like I am and our ragged breathing fills the otherwise silent room. He takes a deep breath while tensing his jaw before opening his eyes again and putting me back on the ground.

He turns his head to the side avoiding my gaze. "You've no idea how long I've wanted to do that." His voice is low almost like he didn't intent for me to hear it, but with my newly heightened senses it sounded clear as ever.

He turns around fully, now with his back facing me and I try to steady my breath while I look at him with confusion. Why did he stop so abruptly?

"You need rest for tomorrow." He's louder now and back to his commanding tone.

"As do you." I retort still a bit out of breath and perplexed by everything that just happened. It hasn't fully sunk in yet.

He doesn't turn around at my response. "Very well, I shall let you get some rest." He begins to walk towards the door and something in me panics. I don't want him to leave yet and be alone...

"Wait!" I say urgently and he stops dead in his tracks.

I blink a few times not sure what to say now that I've gotten his attention, and he stands still waiting for my words that I've yet to find.

"I'm... nervous about tomorrow." I sound shaky.

Legion finally faces me again. "What about?" He asks like it's unfathomable that there's anything I could possibly be nervous about. It didn't take long for him to turn to back into stone it seems.

I huff and look around in disbelief. "Everything." I state dumbfounded by his question.

He crosses his arms, clearly contemplating my response. "You'll do good." He tries to reassure me, but fails.

I roll my eyes and walk towards the bed ignoring his response. Once I've reached the bed I practically rip away the covers in an attempt to show my annoyance. I get into the bed not even bothering to look in his direction. I turn to my side with my back facing him. "Goodnight!" I curtly say.

I don't get a response back. I listen intently waiting for the sound of him leaving the room but much to my surprise he doesn't leave immediately. As I lay there waiting in silence, my fingers find my lips. My lips feel swollen against my finger tips and I shudder remembering why.

Suddenly I hear him move and I drop my hand quickly. Then I realize that he's moving towards me instead of out the door and I freeze completely. In a second Legion is by my side also pulling aside the covers. At first I think that he might rip the covers off me for acting the way I did but instead I feel the mattress dip down beside me.

I turn around confused only to come face to face with the sight of Legion sitting in my bed next to me. "How can I calm your nerves?" He asks with lips more red and plum than normally. I shudder again as flashbacks of those lips on mine appear in my head. He pierces my eyes with his silver gaze as if he knows what I'm thinking about and my eyes widen in shock.

CHAPTER 14 - TENSIONS

I awake suddenly, confused and groggy. My eyes slowly blink open as I hear the faint sound of Marisa's voice through the door along with knocking. "Your Highness." It almost sounds like she's singing.

My eyes shoot open and I instantly sit upright startled by my sudden awakening.

It's morning?

My face contorts into a confused expression as I try to recall last nights events. A hot flash runs through my body as I remember soft lips colliding with mine, then it ending abruptly. Then there was some anger and I got into bed.... As did Legion!

Startled I whip my head around scared to see what I'll find. Much to my horror, my eyes are met with the large figure belonging to Legion.

All color drains from my face as I realize that he has slept next to me in the bed, currently with one of his arms wrapped around behind me.

How did I not notice that until now!?

"I'm coming in!" Marisa continues as I fail to respond.

At this my head peaks up again. "No no no wait!" I say loudly and Legion stirs awake besides me.

"Oh hush I'm entering."

By the time I register Marisas words, the door creaks open and I know it's to late. At the same time Legion sits up casually not seeming bothered.

Marisa stops dead in her tracks upon seeing us in bed together and gasps as her eyes flicker between us.

"You rule breaking little rascals." Her lips form a huge smile with the usual teasing glints in her eyes.

"It's not what it looks like!" I stress as I hold up a hand to stop her from venturing further into her assumptions.

Legion sighs and gets out of bed in a shift motion then he corrects his somewhat disheveled clothes. "Don't mind Marisa she simply loves some good gossip." Legion tries to reassure me as he runs his hands through his unkept hair, trying to get it slicked back.

For a short moment my eyes linger on his messy hair and I feel some color return to my face along with heat, but the moment is short lived as Marisa replies.

"I mean this is hardly gossip, I caught you red handed." She sounds ecstatic and I drop my head in my hands now feeling heat rise to my cheeks for a different reason than the sight of Legions messy hair.

"Marisa, put a dimmer on your delusions please." Legion sounds assertive but as I've witnessed before it never intimidates Marisa so it's pretty much pointless, which is proven correct as she giggles.

"I won't tell, let's just hope you didn't mark her yet or she'll have to wear a scarf today." I peer through my fingers still too embarrassed to face them, unfortunately she notices it and sends a wink my way.

I groan and get out of bed, hoping that my fully dressed state might be an indication that we're telling the truth, however I doubt anything could change her mind at the moment.

Legion simply ignores Marisa as he brushes his hands over his clothes, while Marisa throws suggestive glances my way.

"Willow." Legion says, not giving Marisa any more attention, he directs his full attention to me. "I look forward to the ceremony and I hope the feeling is mutual." Though his voice is huskier than usual this early, I can still hear the slightly hopeful tone in his voice. Unfortunately my mouth is still glued shut due to Marisa wiggling her eyebrows at me which is very apparent from the corners of my eyes, making me unable to formulate any coherent sentence.

He catches on quickly as he looks at his cousin and send a nod my way, "very well. If you need anything let me know." With that he leaves the room while my eyes widen slightly at his kind offer. It feels like the first time he's said anything like it... perhaps yesterday changed something between us?

I'm quickly drawn out of my trance as Marisa steps in front of my line of view looking all giddy. "I want all the details!"

"It's your cousin." I state with a deadpan look.

Her face changes slightly into a more serious look. "Oh right some-times I forget I'm related to that grumpy man." She flashes me a sorry smile and I exhale, feeling off the hook.

"Not so fast, you still have to tell me everything that happened at least. But... spare some details of course." She regains her devious expression.

I groan and fall back into bed.

●~•~●~•~●~•~●~•~●~•~●

There wasn't much to tell Marisa. I left out the part where we kissed and just jumped straight to the part where I was worried about today and he got into bed with me to answer all my questions about the ceremony, somewhere amidst all my questions I must've fallen asleep and I suppose Legion must've too.

She didn't believe me and immediately began searching my neck for marks. This got me worried as I remembered Legions lips against my neck, thankfully she found none. This revelation made me shudder however as I realized that Legion was holding back on me last night. I began to wonder what it would feel like if he wasn't holding back at all while Marisa was questioning me, which made concentrating quite difficult.

Marisa seemed disappointed that nothing had happened yet she still didn't believe me. I of course couldn't tell her that she was right and especially not about the kiss as I was still processing that part myself.

I sigh but my sigh feels heavier than usual now that I'm surrounded by the water in my bath. Marisa had one of the women draw a bath for me, as a start to my 'special day', like she put it.

The pressure from the water feels both comforting due to the significant slowing of my heartbeat but it also feels suffocating as the weight of the water almost makes it harder to take complete breaths.

I close my eyes as I try to recall some of Legions answers.

The whole castle will be there.

An elder will ask you questions.

A crown will be placed on your head.

Elders will perform an ancient ritual.

I submerge my head under water to escape my restless mind but quickly give up as it just makes my thoughts and anxieties sound so much louder in the silent water.

I fully give up on trying to relax and exit the bathtub. The long mirror in the bathroom is fogged up but I can still see my bare silhouette in it's reflection. As I stand there looking at myself another thought appears in my head.

Am I good enough to be a queen? A Luna? Anything but myself?

I lean further into the mirror as I direct my attention to my face, a flashback of yesterday rush through my mind and I gently touch my lips where his lips once were.

Is it crazy that I want more of that?

A gentle knock sounds at the door and I quickly pull away from the mirror and wrap myself in the soft robe on the counter.

"Yes?" I respond.

Marisa peaks her head in, "oh good you're done." She fully opens the door to reveal a whole staff of women behind her.

"Yeah..." I say as I cross my arms over my chest suddenly feeling rather exposed.

•~•~•~•~•~•~•~•~•~•

"Your hair is gorgeous Your Highness, I've never seen white hair on such a young lady, and never this shiny." The woman doing my hair gushes as she finishes putting my hair in a beautiful updo with impressive braids tangling together to create a masterpiece. "It almost looks like it's glowing."

"Thank you." I timidly say as I stare back at myself in the mirror. My hair has always been a sore subject for obvious reasons.

"And so long too... it reaches your waistline." She sounds awed as she continues and it almost seems like she's speaking to herself so I simply flash her a smile, hoping that I don't seem rude. The lady doesn't seem to mind my silence however and simply continues with the finishing touches as she places all sorts of jewelry in my hair.

"My my, it looks like you're about to faint." Marisa interrupts as she looks at me through the mirror. "Perhaps we should go for a walk and catch some air?" She suggest and I'm quick to nod.

The room seems suffocating with all these women trying to prepare me for the ceremony. Though I'm dressed properly now I still feel self conscious. Perhaps it's because I know I'm about to become their Luna and Queen.

"I'm also finished now Lady Gryphen." The woman says and I exhale in relief as I get up.

"Shall we?" I ask impatiently.

Once we're outside the room Marisa interlocks her arm with mine. "Are you alright?" She sounds concerned.

I try to look more relaxed than I am as I answer. "Of course, I'm just nervous about today is all."

"I understand today is the day we've all been waiting for afterall." Her voice is brimming with happiness now and I can't help but notice that it is a little contagious as I feel something flutter in my heart. Perhaps I'm also slightly excited? Or maybe just nervous...

Before I can reply Marisas expression drops slightly.

"Hello Ladies." I spin my head in the direction of the voice. I'm met with Caspian's overly friendly smile as he looks at me. "Your Highness." He nods his head in my direction and then in Marisas. "Lady Marisa Gryphen."

"Caspian Winterbourne." She says as she tugs on my arm ensuring that I don't make a stop to greet him.

Confused by the interaction, I take a peak over my shoulder. Caspian has stopped walking and is now peering our way. He's smirking as our eyes briefly connect and I quickly twist my head back around, praying that I wasn't too obvious.

We walk further and once I'm sure that there's enough distance between Caspian and us, I speak up. "What was that about?"

Marisa exhales as she continues our stroll through halls I've yet to see before. "Although he may be Legions cousin, believe it or not, we never got along." Marisa shrugs.

My eyes widen. "You? Not getting along with someone? I find that hard to believe, how can anyone but love you." I state sounding surprised.

"It's more that I don't like Caspian." She sounds more somber than usual and I decide to push a bit for information, because of how the dinner yesterday went. The unspoken tension between Legion and Caspian still has me perplexed.

"Does this have something to do with Legion?" I try to not sound so eager and instead slow my speech so it doesn't sound like I'm pushing to hard.

"Besides the fact that he seems fake towards me, yes. Caspian hasn't made it easy on Legion. When Legions father died-" my heart automatically picks up it's pace at the mention of King Octavius. "-he began questioning Legions decisions as king and even called him unfit for the title."

I raise my eyebrows, shocked that the man who just greeted us with such a huge smile is hiding that side of himself beneath his friendly facade. "That sounds horrible."

Marisa nods in agreement. "And you'd think he would've been more supportive as he himself has lost his father."

I turn my head towards Marisa with a quick jerk. "What?"

Does death follow this family or something?

"Legions uncle Kaden, the old king." Marisa replies as if it's common knowledge, and perhaps it is but back in my village my mother and I usually stuck by ourselves and I barely knew of life outside my village.

I just keep looking at her with a puzzled look and she eventually gets the message that know nothing of this.

"Ah you didn't know. Well King Kaden died when Caspian was just five in a battle, causing King Octavius to get the thrown as the second in line." Her voice has fully lost its usual spark now as she speaks of the tragedies in the kingdom.

"I see. That must've been hard on Caspian."

"Indeed so you'd think he would've been there for Legion when his father passed but instead he began questioning everything that Legion did and his integrity as the new king, saying that he was to young to rule." Marisa leads us down the stairs I originally ascended when I first came to the castle and where I first met her.

"Why do you think he did that?" I ask baffled by all the new information.

Marisa looks lost in thought for a moment taking in my question as a silence surrounds us. I scan the castle confused by the silence as I usually hear snickers and whispers but the castle is empty. I suppose everyone are getting ready for tonight as not a single soul can be found in the near vicinity no matter what halls she drags us through. I take a moment to appreciate the peace of not being starred down with every step I take, while Marisa continues to lead us. My peace is disturbed instantly though as the vacant halls only confirm the soon-to-be ceremony.

Thankfully I'm ripped out of my thoughts as Marisa finally replies. "Perhaps envy, perhaps tough love, I can't say Willow but I do know one thing and it is that no one treats my family like that." She finally stops walking and I turn my head forward. In front of us are two ginormous crimson colored doors. "And now that you're part of the family, you'll always have me." She knocks on one of the tall doors that seem never ending. I look around, I hadn't noticed that this part of the castle is so big that I can't even see any resemblance of a ceiling.

The doors open wide as two servants pull on each door and a red tinted light shines brightly in my eyes as I'm greeted with the beautiful view of what I presume to be the ceremonial room.

The room is colossal with an aisle running down the middle of the dark floors. The floor looks like dark marble, which creates a shiny look, almost as if the floor is all wet. There are countless seats on each side of the aisle, and each wall is accompanied by several statues with strength exuding from them. They all depict the Moon Goddess.

At the very end of the aisle sits a beautiful throne on top of an elevated platform. There's a balcony behind the throne which is very visible due to the huge glass windows behind the platform.

There's also a large window over the throne in the hidden ceiling shinning a bright light onto the throne, illuminating it. Not even to mention the smaller windows scattered throughout the ceiling, however they're red stain-glass windows, which is also the source of the mystical red color that fills the room.

I gasp as I take in the sight before me.

———————————————————————

Thank you thank you thank you for your patience. As I continue to travel my time continues to be limited I'm so sorry! :(

However the whole story is mapped out so have no fear, just have patience;) hehe

What did you think of this Chapter? Getting excited for the ceremony?

Are you liking this side of Legion and Willow?

Do you think Caspian is being too rough on Legion?

How do you think you would've handled the encounter with Marisa in the morning lol?

As always, click the star! Comment! And stay safe<3

Chapter 15 - Ceremony

Since arriving to Legions kingdom, I've yet to see the castle as guarded as it is today, however so open at the same time. I suppose that is the reason for the large number of guards.

The great doors to the castle are wide open today, leading a never ending stream of people from the entire kingdom inside.

These past days leading up to the ceremony, I've had constant flares of anxiety however nothing quite like the feeling I have now, standing on my balcony peering over the many people bustling to get inside the grand halls of their kings fortress.

I'm thankful that no one has spotted me looking over the crowd, they're far to busy trying to soak in as much of the castle as possible. Thankfully with a castle as big as this, I'm nothing but a mere dot in the grand scheme.

As much as I'd like to tell myself that they're just here for Legion, I know I'd be wrong. They are here for me just as much, if not more. Here to see their new queen and luna. The looming dread thickens and I sigh as I step away from the balcony, distancing myself from the tormenting reminder of my newly gained popularity.

It was just a few weeks ago I was a nobody in my village, just another face in the crowd. But now I'm faced with responsibilities I never even thought imaginable for me.

"You're pouting." Marisa points out, shooting me a disapproving glare.

"I am not... I'm simply thinking." I say in my defense, which technically isn't incorrect.

She tsks at me and directs my attention to the white ceremonial dress that she's prepared for me to put on. "Robe off." She commands.

I roll my eyes. "Yes my lady."

"You're going to take their breaths away." She turns around allowing me to losen my robe in privacy and then I step into the dress. "I'll be surprised if a few of them don't faint all together at the sight of you." She exclaims and turns back around just in time for me to hide my body away under the still loose fabric by clinging it to my chest.

"Allow me." She walks behind me, making sure not to step on the any of the white fabric, before she starts tightening the dress by pulling the laces. "The ladies did a splendid job on this dress, it fits you like a glove."

She tugs until my lungs feel constricted. "Which reminds me, we should get gloves for the outfit!" Marisas words basically trip over one another.

"Easy, I'm the one who's supposed to be stressing." I calmly state and turn around to put my hands gently on her shoulders. "And... I think I'll do without gloves, thank you."

She exhales nervously. "Of course, I'm being silly." She runs a hand through her hair looking somewhat nervous as well. "I Just want this day to be perfect, for you, for Legion, for the whole kingdom even."

I attempt to swallow a lump that's formed in my throat before facing the mirror in front of us. "Me too..." I say as I stare at my timorous reflection.

•~•~•~•~•~•~•~•~•~•

Once again I stand before the infinite doors in red only this time the room beyond them isn't empty.

"Your Highness?." One of the guards in front of the doors questions, silently asking if I'm ready to walk in.

I shake my head, not quite ready yet. The guard nods his head curtly and goes back to avoiding eye contact with me. I scan the hall in which I'm waiting, it's filled with at least ten guards. It should comfort me but it doesn't... I can't help but feel that there's a reason for the amount of security needed.

"Excuse me...?" I direct my attention at the guard who had just spoken to me not to long ago and he looks back at me with confusion until he finally understands my intention of learning his name. "Elex." He finishes my sentence.

"Elex, how come there's so many guards today."

He looks taken aback, I don't know if it's because I'm speaking directly to him or because my question hit a nerve but either way he replies somewhat with confidence. "Your Highness, it is because the King has ordered for us to keep you safe."

The answer is just as I suspected and I lower my head slightly as an odd feeling of disappointment spreads within me, as if I wanted the answer to be different and perhaps reveal some secrets, so I press on. "But isn't this a bit excessive?"

"I doubt the King has limitations on your safety Your Highness." He looks at me with slight confusion like he doesn't understand why I'm questioning these matters.

"Of course, you're right, I'm just nervous." I say with an awkward laugh and the guards face lightens a bit.

I redirect my attention to the doors in front of me and take a deep breath whilst closing my eyes. Not a single sound has escaped the room, if I didn't know better I'd think it was empty. I reopen my eyes and step towards the doors. "I'm-" I begin but my voice cracks and a strong sensation of nausea overtakes my senses.

The two guards in front of the doors look at me expectantly so I try again and nod my head. "I'm ready."

With that they push upon the large crimson doors and unfortunately they open quicker than I had hoped.

I hear several gasps from within the room but I can't see anything yet due to the radical light difference. It is dark in the ceremonial hall and it takes my eyes a few seconds to adjust and by the time I can make out the scene in front of me, the doors have fully open and it's time for me to walk down the long aisle.

I quickly try to recall what Marisa and I practiced earlier.

Walk down the aisle.

Stand next to Legion.

Simple...

My body moves involuntary before I get a chance to overthink it, as if it has a mind of its own yet again, perhaps my body doesn't want to be humiliated or perhaps I'm drawn to my mate but either way I'm grateful.

As I move as much as the dress allows, hopefully looking somewhat graceful. I try to keep my head facing forward, however I do sense the endless stares from all around even if I can't see them.

Thankfully my shoes are without high heels, despite Marisas many protests against it, minimizing my chance for falling by quite a bit.

I can't spot Legion yet, the light from the hall I had just waited in disrupts my vision in this dark room so instead I daringly shift my eyes to look around subtly.

The room is lit up with more candles than I've ever seen in my life, it's truly beautiful. As my seeing sense is activated so is my other senses that had earlier been tampered with by my nausea.

Magical tunes reach my ears. A choir must be singing from somewhere within these walls along with musicians who are playing on harps.

The soothing sounds work their magic to calm me but just as I find some sort of comfort in their embrace the invasive sound of doors closing behind me reach my ears. I jump slightly but keep moving nonetheless, hoping no one saw my reaction.

Now that the room is fully darkened, it suddenly comes to life. The shiny marble floors, the red tint of the room, the never ending seats- now occupied by way to many people for my liking- it's as it was earlier.

The windows above are also as they were before except now the moon is shining through and not the sun. This comes to my attention shortly before I step into the light casted in front of me by the moon beaming through the window onto the rest of the aisle.

The more I move into the light the brighter it seems but when I tear my eyes away from the powerful moon, it becomes clear to me that it is in fact me who is being illuminated, to be more specific, the dress I'm wearing. It must be made with some sort of fabric that makes it glow when the moon graces it.

The gasps around me yet again confirm my fears: I'm now fully visible to everyone as I walk down the aisle in the shine of the moon.

The nausea returns with tenfold. Perhaps they're noticing that I'm not normal! Is my hair to easy of a giveaway?

My thoughts end there as my eyes are drawn to a pair of alluring silver eyes. These are the familiar eyes that draw me in like none other and my brain has quickly replaced whatever worry I had with a goal to reach Legion.

He stands tall on the platform in front of the balcony looking striking with the glow of the moon emanating from behind him.

He is wearing a black suit, one that only royals wear. It looks like something only a true king would wear, it's magnificent. Under his black coat is a dark blue shirt with white embroidery, it's hard to take my eyes off the intricate details of the design.

My eyes wander more exploring the man ahead of me. His black hair is slicked back however a lose strand does find itself lost as it hangs over his eyebrow. On his head sits a golden crown with all sorts of riches adorned on it. It's stunning beauty fits Legion and it leaves me momentarily breathless.

The closer I get the more clear it becomes that Legion isn't planning on letting me out of his sight any time soon, his eyes are fixed on me, studying even the smallest details about me.

My legs start to feel wobbly but not because I'm nervous it's because I can tell that Legion is delighted underneath his hard exterior. I doubt anyone can see it but me. To others he probably looks like their usual steadfast King. To me however he looks like so much more.

The weight of the dress suddenly doesn't feel so heavy anymore and before I know it I'm right in front of the platform and Legion, looking up at him through my lashes with an unwavering gaze that's shared between the two of us.

He reaches a hand out in front of me, offering me support to get up the few steps in front of me, all the while the music plays on.

I slowly grab his hand and I'm instantly overcome with a warm electrical feeling, one I never seem to get used to no matter how many times we touch.

He thankfully steadies me as I timidly walk up the steps, all the while never breaking eye contact with me. I wonder if I even would've been able to get up here if it wasn't for his hand. Even once I've reached my place next to Legion his hand lingers on mine.

It's not until the music stops that he lets go of my hand. I instantly find myself longing for his touch again and a blush spreads across my cheeks.

Legion takes notice of this as his eyes briefly shift to my pink tinted cheeks. I take that as an opportunity to finally break the eye contact between us and instead direct my attention to the big crowd of people in front of us.

My heart begins to race as I realize that they're all standing up, looking at us expectantly. At me. Scanning the crowd I try to look for familiar faces. In the front rows sits many noble looking people, amongst them is Marisa and her mate. She smiles to me and mouths something that looks like 'breathe'.

I follow her advice and take a deep breath, but it does just about nothing to calm me. My eyes travel further which I quickly regret as I spot the face of Cathrine two rows down, she looks anything but amused so I hurry my eyes along.

Soon enough they land on another familiar face, Caspian. He isn't smiling but he doesn't look unhappy or angry either. His expression is rather blank. For some reason that makes my skin crawl so I advert my gaze.

Just as I do this an elderly woman steps forward from seemingly nowhere. Her hair grey with small strands of white and black. She's wearing a black dress that looks ancient, as if it's from a different time. I wouldn't call it beautiful, I'd call it striking, like it demands respect and attention.

She initially faces the crowd and everyone but me and Legion bow their head in respect before all sitting down. Then she turns to Legion and me, slowly walking up the steps.

The elderly lady stops right in front of me, her eyes scanning mine as if trying to stare into my soul. She then reaches her hands out to grab a hold of mine and I stall for a bit unsure of what to do until I catch on and shakily put my hands in hers.

She closes her eyes and starts whispering something to herself. I look at Legion with wide eyes but he simply nods reassuringly. Once I return my gaze to the lady her eyes are already open and on me, which makes me internally jump.

With no further notice she swings back around to face the crowd and walks a few steps in front of Legion and me.

"This young lady is the true mate of our Alpha, King Legion Winterbourne." The elderly lady speaks loudly for the whole crowd to hear.

I peer over the crowd for reactions, but everyone simply seems to be listening intensely to what she has to say. Though I'm happy to see that most of the people seem to look joyous.

"The blessed kingdom of the north has gathered here today under the watchful eye of the full moon to bear witness to the crowning and acceptance of our new Luna and Queen, Willow Ashen." The lady's voice is clear and loud, even powerful but also worn out due to years and years of using it.

She's got everyone's attention completely captivated, including mine. The elderly woman then starts walking once more and we all follow her with our eyes as she makes her way towards Legion.

As the elder stands in front of Legion, I can't help but notice Legions impressive stature next to the short and shrunken woman. He's practically double her height and more than double her frame. I nervously exhale a breath a didn't even realize I had held.

Legions eyes swiftly meet mine for a few seconds, almost knowingly, before returning to the woman.

The woman gestures Legion forward and he complies with certain steps. Together they walk up to the front of the podium as I stare at the back of his black hair, relived that I'm somewhat hidden behind them.

"Legion Winterbourne, do you, with the weight of your ancestors and the honor of your lineage, accept Willow Ashen as your mate" The woman asks and her question immediately makes a part of me nervous, as if the answer could perhaps be something other than yes.

Legion wastes no seconds however and my fears are quickly subsided. "Yes." He throws a quick reassuring glance over his shoulder or maybe it's to reassure himself that I won't simply sprint away now that it's becoming official.

"Do you accept her as your queen?"

Legion answers immediately with poise as if none of this is unnerving him. "Yes."

The elderly woman nods her head in approval and with that dismisses Legion, who returns to his previous place. Legion locks his eyes with me but I'm distracted as the woman then turns to me.

"Step forward my child." Her voice is lower than before so only I can hear her. I do as she says, hoping that I won't simply faint with all this unwanted attention, as I try my best to ignore looking directly at anyone specific.

Once she's guided us all the way to the edge of the podium, one heavy step after the other, she directs her full attention to me, her gaze penetrating my soul and I sense an instant shift in the air. It's time.

"Willow Ashen, do you with an honest heart accept Legion Winterbourne as your mate." Her voice sends echos through the grand hall, chiming away, waiting to be replaced by my answer.

The air is thick with anticipation. I shakily take a deep breath. Before answering I glance over my shoulder just as Legion had and I'm surprised to see that his eyes seem almost desperate. I turn back towards the woman and let my answer out.

"Yes." My answer strengthens all the threads between us, binding us together with unimaginable force. I know he can feel it too.

A smile graces her lips upon my answer.

"Do you solemnly swear, under the moon's eternal light, to protect our pack, to rule our kingdom with unwavering strength, and to protect your mate forever?"

I peer over the crowd and somehow my eyes land on Caspian almost instantly, his eyes are squinted and he's leaning forward slightly on the edge of his seat. Something about the way he looks at me makes me want to state my answer loud and clear.

"Yes." I say louder than before.

The woman looks at Legion and he responds by moving up next to me.

"As mates, bound by the threads of destiny, know that you shall share your lives from this moment onward. And, when the time comes, you shall also share the eternal embrace of death."

A man wearing fancy clothes walks up to the elder from the side of the hall with a pillow covered in a thin layer of fabric, the pillow is red just like the fabric. The elderly uncovers the fabric, showing the beautiful crown hidden underneath. With reverence, the elder presents Legion with the crown. It looks like it's crafted from moonlit crystal. It's got beautiful gems all over it and a shiny gold base.

"Legion Winterbourne, place this crown upon your queen and mates head, Willow Ashen, and let the world bear witness to the dawning of a new era."

Legion bows his heads bit as he grabs the crown with gentle hands. My heart picks up it's pace as he moves it closer to my head but I'm not looking at the crown, my eyes are transfixed onto Legions silver eyes that are now filled with a glow that wasn't there before, they're practically gleaming.

Time moves in slow motion as the crown is carefully placed on my head by Legion. Everyone and everything around us seems to disappear in that moment.

"My Queen at last." Legion leans closer and whispers in my ear.

My body simmers at his words and I'm rendered speechless.

His lips form a smile, not a smirk but a genuine smile. His hand reaches out to tug a single hair strand behind my ear and I lean into his hand whilst closing my eyes in bliss. I wish this moment would last forever.

Legion doesn't remove his hand but instead starts caressing my cheek. Despite my eyes being closed I'm certain that both is our eyes are glowing.

Then as quick as our moment appeared it's ripped away with the voice of the elderly.

"Long live the King and Queen!"

The crowd repeats after her loudly. I open my eyes and turn towards them as they all stand up and bow their heads in front of us.

"It is time for the fated candles my King." The elderly woman says as more women appear behind her with a candle each in their palms.

Legion nods his head curtly as the women form a semi circle in front of the platform. Legion places a warm hand on the small of my back whilst the elders starts chanting something in a faintly familiar language.

As the woman who conducted the crowing lights the first candle, starting the chain of candle lightings down the line it dawns on me that it's the language I've heard Legion speak.

I watch with attentive eyes as the last candle is lit and smoke starts forming from each candle. The candles all move as if they were one. I lean in perplexed by the sight only to notice that the smoke is forming an unnaturally big cloud above the women.

"The candle shall serve as a fortune." The elderly says in the language I understand. "Look into the smoke my King and Queen, look at your future."

All the women start chanting together and as their voices grow louder and more pressing, the smoke starts forming shapes of all sizes. It's like a moving picture.

I lean further in involuntary, entranced by what's appearing before me. Legion responds by pressing me closer to his side and I allow the comforting action as I remain fixed on the smoke.

The smoke begins forming familiar images, as if controlled by a magic force allowing me to see these visions. At first I see what appears to be a lone woman walking through a forest, as I look at her I feel a sense of vulnerability surrounding her, without knowing why.

Then a mysterious looming figure starts forming behind her, casting a growing shadow right behind her.

Then a man emerges to embrace her. But the looming figure grow taller and more menacing, slowly growing big enough to swallow the pair.

The vision unsettles something deep within me and I gasp as I turn my face away from the eerie vision. Instead I lean desperately into Legions side whilst looking behind us, seeking solace in the moonlit landscape just beyond the balcony. He doesn't turn around like me but his grip on me tightens with every moment passing, securing me in his embrace.

As I try to calm myself down, I overlook the village and even beyond to the distant tree-line where we had originally emerged to reach the kingdom. That's when something catches my eye, a lone figure appears at the tree line. Despite being so far away I'm positive that it sees me just as I see it, and that's when it flashes me an eerie smile.

_______________________________________A/N

I deeply apologize for how long it took, so I've made this chapter longer to compensate little.

As most of you know I've been traveling for months on end but I'm back home now. Sadly enough however I've come down with a fever so the fact that I even pulled myself together to finish the chapter is a miracle haha.

I'm just kidding but I do truly feel just miserable and I'm hoping for a quick recovery!

Now there might be some typos here and there, I'm sorry about that but I figured I can always look it through when I feel better and that way you guys can get the chapter quicker.

What did you think of the chapter?

CHAPTER 16 - AFTERMATH

"You may leave us." Legion says to the two women who helped me navigate the halls with the huge white dress.

They nod politely excusing themselves from the room, closing the door behind them on their way out. I take a deep breath trying to settle my heart rate that only ever seems to malfunction since meeting Legion, however this time it cannot be blamed on him as the image of the eerie smile is burned on the insides of my lids.

Legion unbuttons the one button holding together his royal jacket and takes a seat on a dark blue couch. I proceed to stand out of place in the middle of the bedroom, not fully having processed the night.

"Do you wish for some alone time?" He asks after a moment of silence has passed between us.

That's the last thing I'd want right now, to be alone with my thoughts, so I shake my head probably looking more desperate than intended.

He leans in slightly now with his arms resting on his legs. "Is something the matter Willow?" There's a hint of worry in his voice, perhaps he thinks I have regrets.

I want to answer his question truthfully and explain what's really bothering me. That I don't have regrets but the smoke mixed with the far away smile spooked me. But alas I can't find a way to explain that I thought I saw a shadow that looked so recognizable it made my blood run cold. I also can't tell him that it smiled at me, or that my mind must've played a trick on me. He would think that I was going mad...

I cast out the worries from my mind and instead focus on the man in front of me. Black shiny hair slicked back with a few rouge strands over his forehead. His crown is no longer on his head, same with mine, as they were taken by the elders for safe keeping until we needed them for important matters.

His silver eyes surrounded by black lashes are locked on me as I study him, but my eyes continues to wander to his pink-tinted lips.

I'm officially his mate, his queen...

"Willow?" He breaks my fascination and I become aware that I forgot to answer him.

I shake my head dismissively and look around his bedroom, "all this is just so impressive." I gesture at his room that's somehow bigger than mine. Hoping he'll buy my worn out excuse.

The colors in his room are mostly silver and dark blue, with the occasional black and white.

I can tell by the look in his eye that he doesn't buy my excuse, but he leaves it be regardless.

"A celebratory party will be held tomorrow in our honor, so we best get some sleep." He removes his jacket completely while saying this and then stands up straight, freeing himself from the couch.

In that moment our deal dawns on me, I'm supposed to sleep in here with him. I'd been so caught up with my mind playing tricks on me that I hadn't even thought, let alone prepared myself, for the fact that I'm sleeping next to him tonight.

Although I'm less abrasive about the thought now than I was some days ago but still I feel myself begin to shiver at the mere thought.

I open my mouth to speak, hoping that my voice isn't as shaky as I am. "I don't know if I'm ready..." Much to my dismay my voice betrays me.

His eyes squint for a second."We'll just be sleeping." He replies, somehow knowing what I mean.

I awkwardly avert my gaze and rub my arms. Sleeping next to him won't be so bad... As I've already discovered.

He passes by me but stops for a moment by my ear and says lowly, "when the time comes you won't just be ready."

I turn my head to face him and he continues,"you'll need all of it desperately."

And with that all my lingering fears about the smile dissipate completely and my body heats up in no time as I stare at the floor in embarrassment that he can make my face red with nothing but his words.

Lucky for me, it doesn't seem like Legion expects a reply, instead he goes to uncover his bed from its multiple soft layers of comfort, getting it ready for our shared night. I watch him quietly as I try to recover from my embarrassment. I even begin to wonder what exactly he was referring to, as there are many things I'm not yet ready for.

When he's finished with the bed he starts undoing his dress shirt and I divert my gaze the second I realize.

"You've seen me indecent before." Legions speaks composed as ever.

"Doesn't matter." I mumble as flashbacks of our first encounter and the lake flood my mind.

He doesn't say anything. I stand perfectly still as I listen to the rustle of clothes, scared that any movement from me, might entice my curious eyes to wander.

In my struggle to keep myself from moving, I fail to pay attention to my surroundings and Legion has soundlessly found his way directly behind me before I can even react.

I become aware of this as his fingers snatch a pin from my hair causing some hair strands to fall in front of my face.

My body freezes on its own and my breathing heightens. Is he decent now?

"Shouldn't you get ready for bed?" Legions question hangs in the air unanswered as my brain scrambles for some words. "Or do you plan on going to bed with all these..." he trails off, "decorations."

Another pin is snatched from my hair as if to demonstrate his word.

I shake my head before any words find their way out of my mouth, now feeling more hair loosen with the lack of restraints on it. "I can't get this dress off by myself." I say lowly, inwardly cursing how suggestive it sounds.

Getting into the dress is just as hard as getting out of it, seeing as it's practically sculptured to my body.

His fingers undo another pin and gently loosen other parts. "You need assistance." He simply states as he undoes my hair fully with calm and collected hands.

My hair drapes all around me now, kind of working as a protective barrier between my peripherals and Legion. I take advantage of my limited vision and unfreeze slightly.

Legion's hands run through my hair, discarding any stray pins they find along their way. I close my eyes enjoying the feeling his hands make while going through my hair. The feeling spreads to the rest of my body sending shivers of pleasure through me, until he suddenly stops, pushes my hair aside and instead trail his hands over the back of my dress.

My eyes spring open but I don't move, instead I wait to see what he will do with a pounding heart. His hands dance over the laces for a small moment before they are gone without so much as a trace of them ever having been there.

Then steps are followed and a door is opened. When I dare to turn around I discover that Legion is in fact dressed, but in another less formal outfit. He sends for a maid and in a matter of seconds a maid makes her brisk way into the room.

My face drops. I don't know what I was expecting or what has come over me, but when Legion instructs the woman to help me get ready for bed, then excuses himself and disappears into another room, through a door connected to his bedroom, I find myself feeling slightly disappointed. But why, I do not know.

The woman who's name I also don't know, helps me undo my dress. I tell her I can take it from there. She brings me a nightgown before she departs. Once I'm alone I step out of the dress. Unsure of what to do with the ridiculous amount of fabric, I drag it into the corner of the bedroom hoping that it won't be a bother.

I slip the nightgown on easily. It is a soft pink color and shiny like most of the materials that they give me are. And it's thin just like the robe I wear after a bath. I sigh and cross my arms over my chest. What I wouldn't give for my own clothes right now.

I comfort myself with the fact that Legion is still absent but my comfort quickly turns sour. It's rather cold in this big room, even more so without his presence. It doesn't take long for the scary images from earlier to creep their way back into my head.

My eyes begin to dart around as if the eerie smile could be hiding anywhere, just waiting for me to discover that it was in fact real and not just my imagination.

I shake my head to rid myself of such thoughts but fail as cold chills run through me. Without thinking I head straight for the door that Legion left through. I don't even bother to knock as it feels like I've got a shadow behind me dying to catch up.

I regret my actions before I even come to a halt as Legions eyes spring up to see what has caused the sudden interruption. And I regret not knocking even more as two other pairs of eyes do the same.

It doesn't take me long to realize that one of the men is Finley, with his red-tinted eyebrows raised in shock and a suppressed smile waiting to break free. I recognize the other man as the blonde nameless guy who is one of Legions closest men. His face is the opposite of Finleys, he is certainly not amused, which is clear by his tense features and the fact that he dropped his gaze the second he noticed me.

Legion's expression however is unlike both of theirs. His eyes don't cower nor does it seem like he'll laugh anytime soon. His eyes darken as he takes in the sight of me, rendering him speechless, as it seems I've cut in right in the middle of a sentence, now left unfinished. He looks slightly flustered standing there wordlessly peering at me with surprise painted across his face.

It's excruciating to realize why these men are reacting this way. I could hope it's because I interrupted their meeting, but it's most likely due to my silly excuse of a nightgown, though I'm sure my ill-mannered entrance isn't helping.

My body heats up in no time with every pounding of my heart and I cross my arms over my chest again, desperately trying to hide. I open my mouth to apologize or excuse myself from the room and then leave as quickly as I came.

I don't get a single word out though before Legion has walked away from the wooden desk that they had gathered around, and has placed himself between me and them as a barrier of sorts.

"That'll be all for tonight." Legion tells the men in a stern tone as his arm wraps around me and ushers me out of the room with him.

Just before the door is slammed shut behind us, I catch a glimpse of Finley and the blonde guy exiting another set of doors that looks familiar, without so much as looking back.

Legion let's go and turns to me, his eyes urgent. "What's wrong?"

I shudder as I recall the feeling that drove me to look for refuge. Legions eyes dart around the room in response, checking every crevice.

"Sorry." I start and his attention returns to me with his eyes still alert. "It's not important anymore." I continue.

"The look in your eyes says different." He counters.

I blink a few times, trying to loose the look of fear that's gotten caught in my eyes. "It's silly really-" I try to explain but he interrupts me.

"It's not silly, now tell me." It sounds more caring than his usual commands.

It's almost impossible to defy this side of Legion. The care in his tone makes my mouth move without permission and before I know it, I've explained everything. From the smoke, to the smile and the eerie feelings. Having said everything out loud, I feel even more stupid than I already did and I grimace at my own ramblings.

Legions doesn't share this grimace though, his face remains serious. He also remains silent as his arms raise and then unexpectedly pulls me into an embrace. My cheek gently lands on his chest as confusion overtakes my face. He's hugging me?

My senses are overtaken by his warmth and his blissful scent. His scent has become easier to overlook with a certain distance between us, but this close it's impossible to ignore. I close my eyes and instinctively take a deep breath. It seems I'm not the only one affected by our close proximity as I feel Legion tense up against me.

"I don't understand." I say lowly now leaning into the embrace.

"I think we should sleep." His words do not offer explanation, on the contrary they confuse me more.

Does he think I'm crazy? Does he forgive me for intruding?

As I ponder more questions about his odd reaction he lets go of me. I stumble slightly, not quite ready for it to be over that quickly. But just as I begin to miss the warmth of him, his hand grabs ahold of mine. I gaze at his eyes hoping that they'll revel more of his feelings than he does.

They're no help however as they avoid me all together, starring in the opposite direction. It reminds me of how I avoided looking at him earlier. It doesn't take me long to guess why as I look down at my shiny nightgown.

He leads us towards the bed. "You must be exhausted after the day you've had." He finally faces me again, with his eyes fixed on mine and strained look dancing around in them. Is he also fighting the urge to let his eyes wander, like I was?

Although I'm self-conscious about the nightgown I'm wearing, or lack thereof, I find a strange amusement in the idea of him feeling as I do so often. Therefore I take an uncertain step closer to him. His jaw tenses up in response and I can practically feel my eyes light up.

I take another step closer having a bit more courage than before and speak in a lower tone than normal. "Is something the matter?" My voice comes out more weak than intended. I'm not even sure what my goal is but I gain a reaction nonetheless as Legion closes his eyes harshly like my words sting.

"I'd say you were doing it on purpose if it wasn't for you always being so clueless." He mutters to himself more than me.

Yet again something overtakes me. It's like his reactions fuels an invisible fire. Perhaps the bond between us is still controlling me... but suddenly I crave the taste of his lips again. It's only been a day but I'm already wanting more of him.

I lift my hand to his chest and place it on his heart. I want to know if his heart is also malfunctioning like mine does so often. His breathing speeds up along with his heart rate and I can't help but lift my other hand as well to explore more.

My hand doesn't make it far though before he grasps my wrist, stopping my other hand from touching his chest. Legion stares down at me slowly shaking his head disapprovingly.

"Do you even know what you're doing to me?"

———————————